ROSE OF SKIBBEREEN

...Book Two
...By John McDonnell

Copyright 2013 John McDonnell

PUBLISHER STATEMENT

FICTITIOUS DISCLAIMER

This book is a work of fiction. Any similarity between the characters and situations within its pages and places or persons, living or dead, is unintentional and co-incidental.

Discover other books by John McDonnell on Amazon at amazon.com/author/johnmcdonnell

...DEDICATION

To my wife Anita.
In celebration of our Irish roots.

INTRODUCTION

This is Book Two in the series about Rose Sullivan from Skibbereen, Ireland. In Book One Rose fell in love with a mercurial Irishman named Sean, who followed her to America from Skibbereen, Ireland, but mysteriously changed his name to Peter Morley. Rose and Peter married and had three sons but by the end of the book, on New Year's Day 1900, Rose found that Peter had abandoned her.

In Chapter One of this book Rose is alone in Philadelphia with no prospects to support herself. The story of how she survives in such grim circumstances is filled with drama, heartbreak, unexpected love, and many surprises. It's all set against the backdrop of the turbulent years of the Roaring Twenties and there's bootleg liquor, the birth of the movie industry, gangsters and even the ghost of Rose's long dead Irish mother. And Rose's husband Peter is still lurking in the shadows, making his way in a world that includes everything from the drawing rooms of the wealthy to the back alleys of the underworld, plus the excitement of a budding movie career.

These are characters you'll grow to love as they deal with love, loss, tragedy, and joy in this Irish American romance.

I hope you enjoy every one of the six books in the series, and I am always happy to hear feedback from readers. My email address is mcdonnellwrite@gmail.com — let me know what you think!

To read other books in the series, visit the John McDonnell Amazon page at:

amazon.com/author/johnmcdonnell

CHAPTER ONE

January 1, 1900

Rose awoke in the gray dawn of New Year's Day to the sound of gunshots outside in the street. Her heartbeat quickened with fear at the sound, and she sat up in bed, trying to make sense of what was going on. Then she remembered: it was a custom in Philadelphia for revelers to "shoot in" the New Year by wearing costumes and walking around the city firing their guns. There were crowds of people outside on the street singing and shouting, punctuated by the occasional gunshot.

She relaxed. Everything was fine. She lay back, closed her eyes, and put her hand out to touch Peter's body.

But he was not there.

Once again she sat up and struggled to waken, to get her mind working so she could digest this fact.

He had told her he was singing at a saloon last night and that he would be home late. "Don't wait up for me, my girl," he'd said. "Sure and it will be a late night, seeing as how it's the turning of the New Year and the new century. The boyos will be wanting to celebrate, and I'll have to sing a good deal of the Irish ditties to them. It's late I'll be getting in from all of that business."

But he was not here.

He had always come home before, even if it was at three in the morning or later, and she would feel his big body sliding in to the spot next to her in bed, him smelling of beer and cigar smoke and the oysters or peppered eggs they served at all the saloons.

The smell was not there. It meant that he had not come home at all.

She could feel the panic like an icy claw closing around her neck. Her heart pounded, her breath came shallow.

He is gone; he has left you, her heart spoke, in its deep wordless language.

No, her mind said. Maybe he has simply gone back to the Lancasters' to sleep. Maybe Mr. Lancaster needed him to drive him somewhere, or the family is going on an outing, or. . .

It is New Year's Day, her heart said. *He has the day off. He should be with you and the children, not his employer. He has left you. It was something you knew was coming, no matter how much you wanted to deny it.*

Gone. Her body ached with grief, with the loss of its partner. He had been distant these last few years, it was true, but she still longed for the warmth of his body next to hers. It still made her feel secure to have him there. His body gave off heat like a furnace, and she treasured its warmth.

Now it was gone.

She wanted to lift her face to the sky and scream, to rage at the injustice of the world, to let all the shame and humiliation out in one long roar that came up from her depths. She felt like she had been shipwrecked and she was clutching onto a plank in the middle of a storm and she was choking on the raging, frothy sea, about to drown.

She pulled the sheets about her as if she could hide from the awful fate that had just presented itself to her. What will I do? I'm lost. I'm finished. I'm alone in this mad country, lost in this mass of humanity, and I will disappear without a trace.

Then she looked over at her three boys, crowded together in their bed. They were jumbled together as always, a mass of arms and legs and tousled hair. They were her anchor, her root. They were about to wake up, prodded into consciousness by the gunfire and shouts on the street three floors below.

I cannot fall apart in front of them. I must not.

Maybe he will come back. I will hold onto that, it will help me to stand up and carry on.

She ignored the voice that said: No, he will not come back. Not ever.

That voice was her mother.

She got up and busied herself, the way she always did when things were troubling her. It was best to keep her hands busy, her mind focused on the details of life. Better to throw herself into the details than to listen to the voice, the lilting voice of her mother who came to her always when things were bad in her life.

"Agra, my treasure, you know this world is naught but pain and suffering. The prize is always snatched from our hands before we can enjoy it. You must follow me into the realm of the Good People, the timeless realm where there is no heartache or pain. They are waiting, my treasure."

"Away with you," Rose hissed, leaping from the bed. "I have no time for Good People, not now or ever."

She went over to the sink, poured cold water from the pitcher into it, splashed it on her face, then busied herself with the business of dressing: buttoning and lacing and putting her red hair in a bun. She stood back from the cracked little mirror on the wall and appraised her face, with its skin that was pale like parchment, the lacework of tiny lines in her forehead, the girlish light fading everywhere but in the sea green eyes. There, despite everything, was still the light of hope.

She sighed. "You'll win no beauty contests, Rose Sullivan, but you'll do."

Then she got the boys up.

"Where is our father?" Tim said, rubbing sleep from his eyes. "And why is it so cold?"

"Your father is working at the Lancasters'," Rose said. "He said something about them visiting their friends on the occasion of the New Year, and he is needed to drive them about. And as for the cold, why, it's simply because it's winter, silly boy. Did you expect a blazing sun on the first of January?"

"No," Tim said, shivering in his thin cotton night shirt, "but I thought we'd have some heat. What happened, did you not pay for your portion of firewood again?"

Rose blushed in embarrassment at Tim's ability to cut right to the truth of the matter. She had neglected to pay Mrs. Cleary, the landlady, for this week's allotment of firewood for the stove and the little fireplace, and so the rooms were almost as cold as the street outside.

"I must have forgotten," she said. "Get dressed now, and run downstairs to Mrs. Cleary's room and buy some wood. I'll give you the money." She went in the kitchen cupboard while Tim got dressed and she found the little jar in the back, the one where she kept spare money, and she opened it and pulled out a few coins. There were three dollar bills in there and some spare change, and it was all she had to buy food with until she finished the lacework on a christening dress and got paid. Cold fear gripped her stomach again, but she ignored it and strode back into the bedroom and gave the coins to Tim.

He had changed into his shirt and pants and was sitting on the edge of the bed lacing his shoes, but it was obvious he had been having a hushed conversation with Paul and Willy, who looked worried. When they saw Rose they stopped talking. Paul gave Tim a playful shove as a diversionary tactic, but little Willy couldn't hide the worried look on his face.

When Tim was gone and the boys were eating their pieces of stale bread dipped in a saucer of milk (for Rose had nothing else to feed them), Paul said, "I think it's time for me to get a job. I'm almost ten years old and I've had enough of school. I'll go to work at the paper mill down by the river. They hire boys my age, and I bet I'll make fifty cents a day there."

"Don't talk nonsense," Rose said. "You'll not be leaving school, young man."

"Why not? I don't learn anything in that school anyway. Nothing except how to fight."

Rose had to agree that fighting was a big part of the curriculum at St. Albert the Great school, where the boys went. It was a German parish, and they didn't fit in there, with their Irish last names and their red hair among all the blonde German boys. She'd had to send them there because the Irish parish, St. Malachy's, would have been worse. Every Irish family in the parish knew that Rose Morley's boy Tim was born out of wedlock, and he'd have been teased unmercifully for that fact. So, she'd made up a story to tell the German pastor of St. Albert's that her husband was part German on his mother's side, and she'd sent the boys to the German school. It was only a slight improvement, however, because they were treated as outcasts by the German schoolchildren, and many days Tim or Paul would come home with marks on their faces from fights they'd gotten into.

"Mother, I can help us," Paul said. "Please let me do it. Tim and I could both work there, and then at least we'd have enough to eat. Most nights we go to bed hungry, and little Willy is always sick."

It was true, Willy had always been a sickly child, and Rose was constantly worried about his health. Even now his skin looked pale, and he had a cough that wouldn't go away.

Tim came banging up the stairs and through the door with an armful of firewood, and he put it in the basket by the door, then came into the kitchen.

"Tim, I have a grand idea," Paul said. "Why don't we go down to the paper mill and get jobs? We could have a great time working there, and make some money to boot."

Tim sat down at the kitchen table, his thick eyebrows knotted, his mouth a tight little angry line, and said, "Why do we need to do that? Is Father not coming back?"

"Now, what would make you say such a thing?" Rose said, her heart jumping in her chest. "Of course he's coming back. I told you, he had to work today. The Lancasters are out visiting all their grand friends and Father has to drive them about."

"He never worked before on New Year's Day," Tim said.

Rose noticed his fists were clenched in his lap. He was a tight little ball of tension, and she wanted nothing more than to go over and stroke his hair and tell him things would be all right, but she knew from experience that would only make him angrier. He did not want her comfort; he wanted his father's strong arms, his father's hearty voice and the pat on the back that made you feel you were an important part of his world. Peter Morley could light up a room with his smile, and he always acted like he was delighted to see you.

"I know he never worked on New Year's before, but that doesn't mean he can't do it today," Rose said. "Things change, my boy. The world does not stay the same, no matter how much we want it to."

"He's not coming back," Tim said, folding his arms across his chest. "You're lying to us."

"Of course he's coming back," Paul said, as usual playing the role of mediator. "Father always comes back, and he will do it again. But in the meantime, Mother, why don't you let Tim and I help you out? We could make a little money, so you won't have to stay up late working on those lace dresses, and we'd be able to feed little Willy better. I don't need any more schooling, and neither does Tim. We can read and write and do our numbers, so what more is there to learn?"

"Yes," Tim said. "All we do is fight at that school anyway. I'm tired of smacking around those stupid Heinies."

Rose looked across at their earnest faces and wanted to cry. She had always tried to hide the worst from them, but somehow they knew that Peter had left, and now they wanted to help. It was true that some other boys their age went to work, but they seemed so young! She had wanted them to get an education, so they would have a better life, and now that would not happen.

And yet, she knew that if she did not get some income, she would be out on the streets with her family. She already owed two month's back rent to Mrs. Cleary, and soon enough the woman would be banging on her door demanding payment.

There was no alternative.

"I'll take you down to the mill tomorrow," she said. "And we'll see about getting you jobs, but only for a little while. I'll find more young mothers to buy my dresses, and you won't have to work there long."

CHAPTER TWO

December 31, 1899

He was James now. It had come to him when Edith asked him his name. It had just popped out of his mouth, as natural as you please. To cast off the old name and the old identity was as easy as taking off an overcoat. He had gone into the city on the afternoon of New Year's Eve, and he'd met Edith Jones at the train station, then spent a magical afternoon with her visiting the shops as she bought her food. They promenaded around the town and he created word pictures about the wonders of life in Philadelphia. "Do you know this was where the old boys signed the Declaration of Independence? Why, they even have a copy under glass. It's a grand country, isn't it? Have you seen one of the new motor cars yet? I rode in one, and it's the most amazing thing for getting you around — it will make the horse obsolete, I predict. Did you know there is a man named Siegmund Lubin who makes moving picture stories? He has developed a machine that can take pictures of people singing, dancing, acting in dramas, just like you'd see in the theater, only they're made of pictures that you can look at again and again."

He was as full of fizz as a bottle of ginger beer, talking in great gusts, lifting her up on a wave of words, like a musician playing just for the sheer joy of listening to the sounds he made. They strolled in the cold, clear afternoon with the crackle of anticipation in the air. The new century was coming! James could hardly contain himself, he was full of such excitement.

He squired Edith around to all the shops, acting like a man of the world, commenting on the latest fashions from Paris in the dressmaker shops as if he had just come from the Continent himself. He treated her to coffee and cake at the German bakery on Broad Street. He showed her the grandstand being put up for the first official Mummers' Parade that was taking place the next day.

Always he talked, the words spilling out of his mouth with abandon, although he never touched on anything to do with his past. It was a high wire act he was playing, keeping her eyes focused on the wondrous show up in the air, making her ignore the darkness below and behind it, the abyss of his past.

He could not afford to let her ask him a single question about himself, because he did not know what he would say. He had not thought of a history to give himself, no life beyond what he displayed to her in this present moment. He was a magician pulling a snow white dove out of his hat and letting her admire its beauty. If she asked too many questions, probed too much, looked inside his coat sleeves, it would be disaster, so he kept her attention focused elsewhere.

It was a glorious day and he felt more alive than he had in several years. Edith looked at him with a glow in her eyes, and he was tingling with excitement, so much that he leaned over and kissed her right there at the corner of Broad and Walnut streets, while they were waiting to cross the street. She lifted her hand like she was going to slap him, but then she smiled at his boldness and he felt exhilarated.

"Mr. Francis you are a bold man," she said. "I daresay you should be slapped, but something prevents me from doing it."

"I am sorry," he said, "but I could not help myself. Please forgive me; I have never acted this way. I have never felt this way."

He had said those words to other women, it was true, but

each time he really meant them. He took her by the hand, and looked down at her with that boyish earnestness that he still had even though he was almost 40. She was trying to be firm with him, but he could see the trembling of her chin as she tried to master herself. They were standing on a crowded street corner and yet he could have kissed her again right there. He felt himself overwhelmed by her beauty, the day, the charge of hope all around him.

When he took her to the train station he kissed her again, on the platform. Her tiny body melted into his, her lips welcomed him and he felt his heart expand once more.

"I must see you again," he whispered when they parted.

Her face was flushed, and she was out of breath. "Mr. Francis, you are the most forward man. . ." she took a big breath, then composed herself, as if she were trying to get her bearings. "I live in Merchantville New Jersey with my brother and his family. I come into the city every Monday and Thursday to buy our groceries."

"I know that," he said, gripping her by the arms. "You told it to me before. Can I see you on Thursday?" It seemed very likely that he would die if he did not see her again.

A train whistle blew.

"My train is about to leave," she said. "I must go."

He gripped her harder. "Edith. I must see you. Will you see me on Thursday?"

"Yes," she said, suddenly kissing him back. "Yes, I will. Meet me here at 12 noon."

He stood on the platform and waved goodbye as her train pulled out of the station, and at that exact moment he knew he would leave Rose. It was like a door had opened in his life and he had to step across the threshold. He had to see Edith again, no matter what, and if that meant his life with Rose was over, so be it. He would close that part of his life like shutting a book.

Walking back from the train station to the subway to go home, he decided he had to seize the moment. It was the end of one century, and the beginning of another. He had to move downstream, let himself be carried by the current, and try for a new life.

He thought about writing a note to her explaining things, and he went to a saloon where he sat down at a table, ordered a stein of beer, and asked the waiter for a pen and paper.

"I must leave you, Rose," he wrote, in his large pen strokes. "The world is changing every minute, and I am changing with it. I am not the same man I was twelve years ago. I am not the same boy who met you so long ago in Skibbereen. I cannot be tied down anymore, I need to keep moving. I am sorry I cannot be there for the boys. They are strong boys, though, and they will find a way to grow up and be men somehow. I did, and I had less of a home to grow up in than them. Goodbye, my Rose."

He felt a twinge of sadness as he folded the letter and put it in his coat pocket. Rose was a good woman, the mother of his children, and he knew she would struggle without him to provide for her. Aye, but they'd still have it better than he did, growing up in Tullamore without a family. Why, he'd been a nothing, a nobody, back then. A ragamuffin who had to scrounge for every morsel of food he put in his mouth. A stable hand for the British soldiers, a messenger boy, a seller of rags and scraps, feeding his hunger with the stems of turnips and the ends of potatoes that nobody else wanted. It wasn't till old Murphy took him in and taught him the way to make poteen that anyone showed the slightest care for him. Things were different here! It was a land of opportunity, a place where anyone could make something of himself, and his boys would have plenty of paths open to them — all they had to do was put one foot down in front of the other, and they'd be fine.

He would mail the letter when he got back to the Lancasters. He had told Rose he was singing in a saloon tonight, and that he'd be home late. It was true that he was singing at a saloon, a place called Garrity's, and he would be singing Irish ballads all night, but he would not go home. He would stay in a room over the saloon, something he had done before, and he would go back to his job at the Lancasters tomorrow evening as if nothing had changed.

He sipped his beer and looked at the men in the saloon, some of them engaged in heated discussions, others thoughtfully staring into space, while the barrel-chested bartender laughed and joked and filled up the mugs with the frothy beer. Are they at peace with themselves? he thought. Do they think about the past at all? Do they carry scars around with them, or memories that wake them in the small hours of the morning? Do they feel this need to keep moving, keep going forward, for fear of the hoofbeats that are gaining behind them?

The answer for him was to run harder. To swallow up the past with the present and future. To pursue the new at all costs. He had told Edith about Siegmund Lubin and his new machine for taking moving pictures. Mr. Lancaster had thought about investing in Lubin's company, and one day he'd had Peter drive him to the Lubin building to see how the machine worked. Peter had seen it with his own eyes, a machine that made moving pictures out of light and shadow, an amazing invention that would allow people to watch dramas the way they did when they went to the theater, or a vaudeville show! It was fascinating, and Mr. Lancaster thought it might have potential. In the end he'd decided not to invest, his natural caution had prevailed. The Lancasters had a past they could be proud of, so they could afford to be casual about the present, could afford to let a moment pass without grabbing it and squeezing the life out of it.

Not James Francis. He had to seize every moment and see what he could produce out of it, like a magician pulling a rabbit out of a hat.

He decided then and there that he would get a job with Siegmund Lubin. James Francis, who used to be Peter Morley, would enter the world of light and shadow.

CHAPTER THREE

January 6, 1900

Rose took Tim and Paul to the paper mill down by the Delaware River and got them jobs, and even though the foreman, a bear of a man named Seamus Draper, said, "Don't worry, missus, I'll look after yer pups," she cried all the way home on the trolley car, clutching Willy to her as if she could not bear to part from him for even a minute. She had worked long hours on the farm when she was the same age as Tim and Paul, so it wasn't that she thought they couldn't handle the work. It was that she did not want them to say goodbye to their childhood yet. "This world is a suffering place for a full grown person," her mother always said. "So, stay young as long as you can, my child."

Her mother's voice was in her head a lot these days. She heard her lilting tones always in the back of her mind, at the edge of her hearing, talking of spirits and fairies and the timeless realm in the glens of Eire.

"They're everywhere, my child. You must only look for them, my precious thing. They sing and dance to the most wonderful music. You can hear it in the wind, my darling, just beyond the edges of your mind. You have only to let yourself go, and you'll hear the music everywhere."

It was so tempting to simply sit by the window, her lacework in her lap, and look outside, to the far horizon where there were green trees, a hazy strip of green beyond the buildings, and dream about the timeless realm, where the beautiful fairy people would take her hand and lead her about in their dances, smiling and bowing gracefully to her. Sometimes she would be so caught up in these reveries that a whole afternoon would pass, and she would forget to start dinner and the boys would come back from the mill with their faces dirty and the stink of wood pulp on them, and Willy would be wanting to tell her about what he learned in school, but they would look at her and say, "Mother, what is the matter?" One day it took her a few minutes to recognize them, and they began to whisper among themselves about her.

She did not keep up with her lacework, preferring to sit by the window and dream. She would lose track of the day and the hour, and would often forget to eat. Her mind was full of so much that it crowded everything in the world out. She got pale and thin, and forgot to brush or tie her hair up, and it was a tangled mass of red curls framing her thin face. She did not like to look in the mirror, because she did not care for what she saw there. The world around her seemed coarse and ugly, and so was the person staring back at her.

One afternoon when she was deep into a reverie it gradually came to her that there was a pounding on the door, and a man's voice shouting, "Rose!"

Who was Rose?

It took minutes for her to realize it was her name. She got up slowly from her chair and made her way to the door. The voice sounded familiar, but she couldn't place it. She stood there with her hand on the door handle and hesitated, wanting to go back to the fairy realm, feeling the pull of unseen forces, but something made her open the door.

There was a man there in a black business suit with a stiff white collar and a worried look on his face. He seemed like someone she should know.

"Rose, it's me, Martin," he said. "Did you not hear me? I've been standing here for ten minutes banging on this door. The landlady told me you were here, but I didn't know why you weren't answering. Are you all right?"

Rose felt strange, it was true, but she still should have been able to answer this kind man. She tried, but it was hard to get her mouth to work. She felt like she was moving in slow motion, and her limbs balked as if she were stuck in mud.

"Rose? Are you all right?" he said again. His brow was furrowed with worry.

She tried to speak again, but no words came out.

"May I come in?" he said.

She wanted to tell him yes, but now she was shaking too much to respond. She tried to take a step toward him, but her knees buckled and she fell into his arms.

He carried her to the couch and set her down gently. Then she was conscious that he had put a wet, cold towel on her forehead, which revived her. Then he left her for a few minutes and came back with a cup of tea. The tea warmed her and cleared her head, and her shivering stopped.

"Are you sick?" he said, feeling her forehead. "No, you do not feel as if you have a fever. You don't look well, though. What is the matter, Rose?"

She moved her lips again, and this time she was finally able to speak. "I don't know. I felt like I was somewhere else. . . just sitting there, thinking of my mother. . . and Ireland. . . my childhood. Do you believe there are other worlds?"

"Other worlds? I don't understand."

"Other places, other people that live all around us. . . a place where there is no sadness. . . where all the people dress in the most beautiful clothes, and they dance to a music that is so sweet and magical. . . like nothing you have ever heard, it is."

"Rose, do you know who I am?" he said. "I am worried about you. Do you know me?"

She blinked her eyes, straining to remember. "I seem to know you. . . I think."

"I am Martin Lancaster. You used to work for my family. Do you remember your husband Peter?"

The name pierced her to the core, and she shuddered, but could not speak.

"Do you know where he is?" Martin said.

She shook her head. "No."

There was a silence. Martin reached out and took her hand. "He has left you," he said.

It was like being thrown into an ice-cold river. She gasped, choked, cried out in shock. She had closed herself off from it, but now it had broken through the membrane of her forgetting.

"No," she said, struggling to keep it away. "No, he has not left. He is just busy. He is driving your father, Mr. Lancaster, somewhere, or perhaps your mother. He has many responsibilities. He sings at drinking establishments, don't you know. To make some extra money for us. He's a very busy man."

Martin squeezed her hand and peered into her eyes. "No, Rose. He is gone. He has left you. I know this because I found a note that he was going to send you. It must have fallen out of his pocket in the carriage. I confronted him about it, and he denied it at first, but then he told me the truth. I am afraid we came to blows over it. My father found out and terminated Peter's employment with our family."

"No, that is not true," Rose said, her breath coming in short, quick bursts. "He will be back to see us this weekend. He will come in the door at half past two on Sunday morning, and he will sleep for a few hours and then we will have a grand Sunday together. Perhaps he will take the boys to the park, or the zoo, or maybe he will take them to get ice cream."

"Do you want me to read his note?" Martin said. "I think

that is what I should do." He pulled a crumpled piece of paper from his pocket, straightened it, and began to read. "I must leave you, Rose..."

She screamed as if someone had stabbed her. Her body shook convulsively, and she gasped for breath as if she were drowning. Martin threw the paper down and pulled her toward him, smothering her anguish in his arms.

She let herself go in his grasp, allowing the river of sadness to overflow its banks, giving over to the deep racking sobs that came from the bottom of her being, while he held her tight. He was an anchor, a plank she could hold onto in the midst of a raging sea, and she clutched at him desperately. He stroked her hair, ran his fingers along her neck, and murmured, "Don't worry, Rose. It will be all right."

She did not know how it happened, but somehow she was kissing him. She had not felt the warmth of love in so long, she had been living in the fairy land of cold, unearthly perfection and now it was like her body was coming back to life, the blood surging through her veins again, her skin tingling like it did when she came in from a winter's day and put her cold hands close to the fire to warm them.

His lips were so warm and tender, and she kissed them greedily, wanting to feel the heat again, the vitality she had been missing for so long. She ran her hands through his thick hair and down his smoothly muscled back, feeling the corded muscles underneath his jacket. His skin was charged, his breath was hot, and she basked in the feeling of excitement, of warmth, of wanting, wanting, wanting with every fiber of her being. She was coming alive after so many weeks in a tomb of ice, a spirit world that had no substance, and she was grasping for life like a drowning woman.

Her heart was pounding as she kissed him again and again, along his neck and behind his ear and all over his beautiful finely hewn face with its sensitive mouth and aquiline nose. The fire caught in him too, and his body quivered with passion as he lifted her chin and kissed her lips, nose, and eyelids with a smoldering fire. He was so gentle, yet so forceful. It was a force born of love, a depth of love she had never felt in Peter, not once in all the years with him, and she could feel Martin's love opening up to her.

"Rose," he murmured. "I have wanted you for so long. Since the time when we kissed in the kitchen so many years ago."

It was a memory Rose had suppressed, because she had been seeing Peter at the time and felt it was wrong to fall in love with her employer's son, a man from a different social class. She had forced herself not to love him, but he had never forgotten, never wavered. She knew he loved her with a deep, pure love, and she gave herself to him with a need and a hunger that she didn't know existed in her.

His fingertips kindled fires in her with every touch, and he moaned in passion, not caring if any of the neighbors in the crowded building heard. A man who was not her husband was inside her rooms with the door closed, and she knew some of the Irish gossips nearby would have noticed. They were scandalized, she was sure, but she did not care. It felt right to be with Martin, and that was all she cared about.

But somehow, he had a cooler head, and he stopped.

"Rose, we should not do this," he said.

"No, no," she whispered. "It's something we should have done long ago, Martin."

"I know," he said, hoarsely, "and I dreamed of this moment for so long. But it is not right."

He put his fingers on her lips, brushed her hair out of her eyes, and said, "I love you too much to let this happen now, Rose. You are distraught, at loose ends. You have been abandoned by your husband, and you are feeling lost. I do not want to take advantage of you when you are in such a state. I love you too much for that."

"But Martin," she said, "I need you now, so very much. I feel like I am shipwrecked, drowning. I need you to save me."

"I will save you, my dear Rose," he said. "I will help you to get on your feet, but I will not take advantage of you in any way. Later, when you are healthy and strong again, I will express my love for you."

Rose was gasping for breath, her heart pounding in her ears, but she somehow got control of herself. "You are right, I know. As hard as it is to stop this, I know you are right."

Martin helped her get up and come to the kitchen, where he made her another cup of tea, and gave her some bread with butter. He watched her eat it, and she was touched once again by the generosity and compassion in his eyes. She felt relaxed with him, and she began to speak. She told him about how she'd had to get jobs for Paul and Tim in the paper mill, how she was so ashamed to make them leave school, how she anguished that she was a bad mother, how she worried that there was not enough money to feed her boys.

"Paul and Tim do not make much money at the mill," she said. "With the little I get for my christening dresses, it is barely enough for us to survive."

"I can help," Martin said. "My mother does a lot of trade with the Wanamaker's Grand Depot store, and my father knows John Wanamaker personally. I will ask them to help you out. I am sure that Wanamaker's could find a position for you, perhaps in the Ladies' clothing department."

"Oh, what do I know about fine ladies' clothes?" Rose said. "I was just a poor Irish serving girl, nothing special."

Martin took her hand in his. "You are a beautiful woman, Rose, and you have intelligence and skill. You would be a fine saleswoman. And you are special to me, so very special." He kissed her hands, then stood up.

"I must leave," he said. "I don't want your neighbors to be scandalized by my presence here. I will be back on Friday, when I have had a chance to talk to my father and mother, and when I have spoken to the people at Wanamaker's. I hope to be able to bring you good news. Take care of yourself, Rose."

He kissed her once more, on the forehead, and then went out.

CHAPTER FOUR

May 1903

Edith had many questions about James Francis, but he stilled them all with a kiss. The man had many mysterious ways about him, but he could make you forget your name when he kissed you.

It was a bit disturbing, really, because Edith felt she should know more about the man she married.

He said he didn't like to talk about his past. "It's over and done with, all gone," he'd say. "No sense dwelling on it, my girl. It has nothing to do with this moment now," and then he'd stop her questions with a kiss.

As a consequence, all she really knew about him was that he was Irish. That alone was enough to make her brother Edward furious, especially when she told him that James Francis had asked her to marry him. "Nonsense," Edward had said. "Out of the question. We don't marry those kind of people in our family, Edith."

But Edith had a mind of her own. She was tired of Edward treating her like a child, tired of living with his whining wife, tired of his children who treated her like a serving girl simply because she'd come over from England to help out when their mother took to her bed with some mysterious stomach ailment (which Edith suspected was not in her stomach at all, but in her head).

It had all become too much to bear, living with Edward and his family, and Edith finally told him she was marrying James

Francis and that was that. When the wedding day came she put on her best blue suit, packed her suitcase, and walked to the train station. She knew she was saying goodbye to Edward, but when she closed the door she never looked back.

She took the train in to Philadelphia, where James was waiting at the station. "My little bluebird," he said when he saw her. "My English bluebird." He gave her that conspiratorial, let's-have-some-fun smile that made her feel she was going on an adventure, and he took her hand in his big paw and they strolled down the street like they had not a care in the world.

They got married at a little Presbyterian church on Walnut Street, and took the train to Atlantic City for their honeymoon. James was an experienced lover, she quickly found that out, and they spent hours in their hotel room, coming out only for dinner and a promenade on the boardwalk in the evening.

James brought excitement, fun into her life. He lit up a room. You simply could not ignore him when he was around. She was never happier than in those first months, when they moved into their little rooms in the Jewish section of Philadelphia. Edith could never understand why James wanted to live there, though. "Why not the Irish section?" she said. "Wouldn't you feel more comfortable there?"

"No, I'm tired of living around those micks," he said. "I came to this country to meet different people and have different experiences, not to be marooned with the same rabble I was with in Ireland."

So they lived in South Philadelphia, amid the pushcarts and the bookshops and the smell of pickles and salted fish in the delicatessen stores. Edith got pregnant within months, and in September of 1902 they had a baby girl, a happy little round-faced cherub that James wanted to call Mercy.

"What kind of a name is that?" Edith said. "Why not a good English name like Susanna or Harriet?"

"I like the name Mercy," James said. "Because she represents God's mercy to me. I am so grateful for her, and I feel my life has changed because of her. That's mercy to me. I could have been a different man if not for this little darling."

He would hold little Mercy in his arms and his eyes would mist up, and he could hardly speak for all the emotion, and Edith would wonder again about his past — what kind of a life did he lead, that he felt so passionately that this baby marked a new beginning for him?

But he closed that part of himself off, and she finally learned not to ask any more questions.

He was a coachman, that is all he told her about his work. He started a new job just before they got married, working for a man named Siegmund Lubin, who owned a manufacturing plant. James came home and talked incessantly about a new invention Lubin was developing, a machine that would take moving pictures. "It will be the next big thing," he claimed. "Bigger than any invention you have ever seen."

Edith liked to be carried along by his enthusiasms, basking in the way his eyes gleamed and his spirit seemed to expand as his stories unfolded. "Why, it's a grand time to be alive, isn't it?" he'd say. He'd point to the baby and say, "Just imagine the wonders that child will see before she dies! It's amazing to think of, isn't it? Why, she might see people walking on the moon!"

Edith would laugh and say, "The nonsense you talk, James Francis!" but he insisted it could happen.

She was happy, even blissfully so, although there were always the nagging questions at the back of her mind. Who was he? Why wouldn't he tell her anything about his past? He kept an olive green steamer trunk at the foot of their bed, and it was always locked. She asked him about it, but he would only say, "It's nothing, my darling girl. Just a few old socks and hats that

I haven't gotten around to throwing away yet. Nothing to bother yourself about."

But she did bother herself about it. She looked at it often and wondered what was in it. Why did there have to be a part of himself that he kept hidden? She had told him everything about her life and family, including her stubborn brother Edward's unflattering opinion of Irishmen, and she held nothing back. She tried to be understanding of his need for privacy, but the steamer trunk captured her till it became almost an obsession to open it. She could not stop thinking about it, and in the daytime when James was at work she would often sit in the bedroom while Mercy slept, and stare at the trunk, trying to imagine what must be inside it.

Then one day the opportunity arose to open it.

James was off at work. His employer Lubin had recently bought a new motor car, called an Oldsmobile, and James was thrilled. "These machines will take over the roads, you watch," he'd predicted. "They're fascinating things, and I want to learn all I can about them."

He drove Lubin everywhere in the machine, although it seemed he spent most of his time repairing it when it broke down. In any case, James was off on a two day trip to New Jersey to visit Thomas Edison's factory, where Lubin wanted to see what Edison was developing, to find out if the famous inventor had anything that could help him in his enterprise.

Mercy was asleep in her cradle when it finally happened. Edith had been thinking about the steamer trunk for days, the idea of it had lodged in her mind and she could not get it out. She thought there should be no secrets between them; they were married, after all, weren't they? There was no reason to hide any part of their lives.

She knew that James had a key somewhere. There was a big brass lock on the trunk, and there had to be a key around. She went to the tall walnut bureau he had and opened each drawer, searching carefully through his clothing, feeling around the edges and corners of the drawer, searching for the key she knew must be there. When she had searched each drawer without success she went to his clothes closet and searched all the pockets of his clothing, even reaching inside his shoes, but there was no key. She was stumped, but it only made her more curious. If he had hidden the key so well, it must mean that there was something very important inside the trunk.

Could it be that he carried the key on his person, perhaps on a chain? No, she had seen him take his clothing off at night, and there was no chain or locket he wore around his neck.

By now Mercy had awakened, and Edith had to forget about her search while she fed the baby. Mercy was almost nine months old and she was a chubby, happy child who had discovered she could crawl. Now, she liked nothing better than to get down on the floor and crawl around.

When Edith had finished breastfeeding her she put the child down and let her crawl about the bedroom floor. She got down on her hands and knees to see what it was like at that level, and for a time she played happily with the baby.

Then, Mercy crawled over behind a lampstand and got stuck between it and the wall, next to the head of the bed. She started to cry in frustration, and Edith went over to rescue her.

It was then that she saw it.

Something gleamed under the bed, catching the sun's rays from the nearby window. She reached under and her fingers closed on something metal. She pulled, and it came loose from the bed frame. It was a key, and it had been taped to the underside of the bed.

She knew immediately what key it was.

She put Mercy down next to the trunk and gave her a small rubber ball to play with, then with trembling hands she put the key in the lock and turned it. There was a click, and when she lifted the top of the trunk, it opened easily.

Her heart was pounding and her breath was shallow and rapid. She lifted the lid and peered inside. At first it just looked like a jumble of clothes and shoes. She rifled through it, not knowing what to look for.

At the bottom there were some old newspapers, and when she read them she saw they were Irish, and they all had stories of some new political development in that troubled land. There were stories of the land reform movement, shootings and bombings by Irish nationalist groups, protests, speeches, calls for independence trumpeted from editorials, and the like. Was this the big secret he had kept from her? That he had an interest in the problems of his native land? That did not seem like something to be kept a secret. After all, she had told him in the past she was sympathetic to the cause of Irish nationalism. It was not something he had to hide from her, to be sure.

But then her hand felt something hard.

She closed her fingers around it, and brought it up to the light.

It was a portrait of a woman and three boys. The boys were wearing sailor suits, and they and the woman stared at the camera with a fierce gaze. The picture was in a brown cardboard frame, and when Edith turned it over, she saw, "To my beloved Peter."

CHAPTER FIVE

December 15, 1905

My dear Theresa,

It has been nearly two years since I last heard from you, and my day was brightened yesterday when the postman delivered your letter.

Then I opened it and saw that Father had died. I had to read that sentence three times before it made sense to me, and I cried bitter tears when the realization of it hit me. It has been so many years since I last saw him. He was the soul of patience, and although he never spoke much I always felt he had a deep well of kindness in him. I remember the smell of his pipe smoke in the house, and how he would sit by the turf fire at night and do something magical with his hands, like carving a whistle out of a piece of wood or making a bracelet for us out of a few old pieces of wire. His face was wreathed with deep creases from working outside all his life, but I remember how it would break into a smile when Mother would sing one of her songs or tell a story. He never lost his patience even when she began to rant about the fairies and the pookas and the banshees, and I knew that he never stopped loving her. He worked hard all his life and though the damp climate gave him rheumatism and his fingers looked swollen and painful and his back was bent by the time I left for America, he never complained.

How much I would like to see his kind face one more time! I left him when I was 18 and I am now 43, and it is a hard thing to know that I will never see him again.

I wish I could have made peace with him, because my last memory of him is of the letter he made you write all those years ago, when

Mary Driscoll told you of my predicament, of my child who was conceived before I was married. I know that Father still loved me in his way, although he did not want to see shame brought upon our family and that is why he told me I was not welcome in the family anymore.

As it turns out, my own family situation has taken a turn for the worse. The last few times I wrote to you I did not want to mention this, but now seems like a proper time. My husband Peter left me several years ago. At first I could not believe it, and I expected him to come back any day, but he never did. I do not know where he is, but I have finally realized that he will never come back.

I asked myself why this happened many times, but I have no answer. He was a man with many mysteries about him, but he never revealed anything, even to his wife and children. I never really knew him, I suppose.

I still see him in the eyes of my boys, Tim, Paul and Willy. They are growing up without a father, and although I love them very much I know I cannot give them everything they need. Tim, the oldest, has an anger in him that frightens me at times. He has grown into a sullen young man who has his father's reckless energy, but in him it has taken a turn down a dangerous path. He drinks too much and consorts with disreputable people, and he has been in trouble with the law more than a few times. He sometimes disappears for days at a time, and he will not tell me where he has been. He gets into fights, and once came home with a scar across his cheek from a knife fight. It pains me to see what is happening to him, but he always had this anger, since he was a young boy.

Paul, his younger brother, is more easygoing. He can be reckless at times, but he has less anger and more control. He wants to make something of himself, and he has already risen to a more responsible job at the paper mill where the boys work. He is the supervisor of the boys on his shift, because the foreman has recognized that he is a leader and that other boys listen to him. I think he will go far in this world.

Little Willy is my baby, and I spoil him still, even though he is 11 years old and tells me he is too big for that. I have lost so much in my life that I keep him close to me, though.

We have struggled much these last few years. It has always pained me that I was forced to let Tim and Paul go to work, because when Peter left I had no money and I was worried we would end up on the street without a roof over our heads. Perhaps because of my guilt over that, I keep Willy close.

I have found work, however, and our lives have gotten better. There is a kind man named Martin Lancaster, the son of my former employer, who helped me get work in a place called Wanamaker's Grand Depot, which is an emporium where people can buy many wonderful things. I work in the Ladies' dress department, and I serve women from the finest families in Philadelphia. They are driven up in their carriages or their new motor cars and they come in and I help them find dresses and gowns for their social affairs.

So, you see, I am doing better than I was before, and I am grateful for my life here.

Now, to the news of our family that you gave me. I am sorry to hear that Brian has gotten involved with the Irish Republican Brotherhood. From what I have read in the newspapers they seem a group that is bent on achieving an Irish state at any cost. They have been linked to bombings and assassinations, have they not? It is disturbing to me that Brian has gone off and joined a group like that. I am as loyal to Eire as anyone but I do not think that bombings and shootings will bring peace to our troubled land. And I fear for Brian's life if he is mixed up with people who do those things. The fact that he has disappeared is worrisome; I expect that he is in hiding because he has done something very wrong.

I am also sorry to hear that our dear Annie has moved away. You say that she has married and moved to Liverpool. It pains me to think that our family is breaking up, but I know that people must go where their heart leads them. Does Annie have no interest in the farm?

I was so glad to read of the latest Land Reform Act, the Wyndham Act that finally made it easy for tenants to purchase the land they have been working for so many years. Because of it, after all those years of being a tenant, of not owning the ground he lived on, Father was finally able to buy the farm last year. Surely, Annie must appreciate that? We have our own land now! That is worth anything, in my eyes. I am still a tenant here in America, and I would give anything to own a little piece of ground. To wake up in the morning and know that you can walk on ground that belongs to you, instead of to someone else — that is surely a wonderful thing. After so many years of being rootless, to have a piece of ground in Skibbereen that is owned by Sullivans, that would make me feel glad, that at least we have something of our own there.

I am sorry that you are alone on the farm now, Theresa. I could tell from your letter that you have some bitterness about that. You speak of a barren countryside, with farms falling into ruin and churches emptied of their worshippers. I can believe you that it is true, for there are so many Irish here it sometimes seems like the whole country has packed its bags and sailed to America. If I could come back to help you I would, but my life is here now, with my boys. I implore you not to lose heart; you can manage the farm with the help of a few hired workers, and it is not too late to find a man to marry. I know there are few enough of them left, but God is good and maybe He will bring a good man into your life.

I feel that I have finally found a good man myself, in Martin Lancaster. He is a kind, decent man who loves me, though I do not know why. He comes to see me every weekend, and tries to help me with the parenting of my boys. Because of him I have been able to manage these last few years. If not for him, I may have been like one of the poor damaged Irish women I see who have lost their husbands to drink or some other calamity, and who scrape along at the edge of poverty with their families, a look of desperation always in their eyes.

Martin has given me hope again, and that is not a small thing.

Because of his goodness, I have joined a small Protestant church here. I know that must shock you, that I have left the faith of my countrymen, but the Catholic church was not a refuge for me in my time of trial. I found no support there, and in fact I was shunned and gossiped about, and my boys were made to feel like outcasts when we walked through the doors of the church. I had to put them in a parish school run by German nuns, because the Irish parish was so unwelcoming.

I am muddling along, Theresa, as best I can. I have made mistakes in my life, that is very true, just as we all do. I hope when all is said and done that I am judged to have been a good person.

And I hope and pray that our family can stay together.

Love,

Rose

CHAPTER SIX

September 1906

Martin's mother was in her element, and she was glowing with exhilaration. Her hair had a silvery tint to it, and it was luxurious in its waves atop her head. The pearls at her neck shone brilliantly, and her dress was of the finest blue Parisian satin and lace. Martin knew the reason she liked this restaurant, the Grimaldi, was because she was sure to be seen by all of Philadelphia's finest, the cream of the city's Society. On the way in to the restaurant she waved to friends and stopped to chat at almost every table. Her musical laugh rang out among the conversations, and she was like a queen bestowing her favors on her subjects.

She clearly was happy to be here, Martin could see, and she had a glow about her when they were finally seated at their table, which had a view of the Delaware River and the barges and sailing ships docked nearby.

But her smile soon turned to a look of puzzlement. "Now, why is it that you asked to see me?" she said, putting her hand on Martin's. "You never meet me for lunch on weekdays. Too busy with your legal work, I know. All of you Lancaster men are such slaves to your work. Your father is the same way. Why, I could hardly tear him away from the office for Victoria's wedding last year!"

"Not so fast, Mother," Martin said, patting her hand. "We've only just sat down. Why not order a glass of wine and we can chat for awhile?"

"You're such a dear," his mother said. "But you know I only drink champagne." She looked at him with a merry gleam in her eyes. "Do you think I should have a glass?"

"Of course," Martin said, summoning a waiter. "My mother and I would like some of your finest champagne," he said to the waiter, an older gentleman in a crisp white shirt and black vest who bowed and went to fetch the bottle.

It was a glorious day in late September, with a crystal blue sky and an opalescent light that made everything look warm and cheerful. It was a day to be conscious of the year's passing, an Indian Summer day, when people were grateful for the reprieve of a few more moments of the sun's warmth before the cold air of winter arrived. Days like this were bittersweet for Martin, because he felt the ticking of Time more intensely, so that even though he told himself to enjoy the moment, he knew there were more moments like this that were in the Past, lost to him forever.

When the waiter came back and opened the champagne bottle and poured glasses for them Martin toasted his mother, saying, "To a great woman, a loving friend and a shining example to me," and took a drink of the bubbly liquid.

His mother's face was flushed, although whether it was from the champagne or the emotion in his toast, Martin did not know. She looked at him with tenderness and said, "Now, Martin, what do you want to talk about?"

Martin still did not want to broach the subject, so he diverted her by saying, "And how is my lovely sister Victoria doing these days? I have not seen her as much since she moved to New York."

"Victoria is doing well, I suppose," his mother said. "Although I do not understand why she has such a desire to get involved in politics. This women's suffrage movement that she has joined seems a bit unbecoming for a person from her background. From what I can gather it is filled with a different class of people."

"Victoria feels strongly that women should be allowed to vote," Martin said. "She feels that women need to have a voice in the running of this country."

"It's nonsense," his mother said, with surprising vehemence. "I think her husband's radical ideas have rubbed off on her. I don't know why she had to marry a man like that, a common schoolteacher."

"He's a college professor, Mother."

"I know, he teaches at some college up there in New York, but still, Martin, I did not expect her to marry someone like that. Your father is a respectable man of business, and that's what I thought my daughter would marry. Not a, a professor of politics or whatever it is he teaches. My word, some of the ideas that man has! Have you heard him talk?"

"Yes," Martin said. "I know he is an admirer of some of the radical thinkers in Germany and Russia. He seems to think that this movement called Socialism has some good ideas."

"I wouldn't say that around your father," she said. "He gets red in the face and his eyelid starts twitching whenever that word is mentioned. He tells me the Socialists think that businessmen like himself are evil. He can barely stand to be in the same room with Victoria's husband, you know that. He almost had an attack of apoplexy when Victoria told him she wanted to marry that man."

The waiter came back and asked if they wanted to order. Martin's mother ordered caviar for an appetizer, and for an entree, Lobster Newburg with asparagus, and potatoes with cream. Martin had simpler tastes. He ordered tomato soup, broiled bluefish and spinach.

He sighed inwardly. Why was it so difficult for him to talk to his mother? He could not even keep the conversation neutral when he tried. All he wanted was to distract her while he gathered the courage to tell her of his future, and now he had her all worked up about Victoria. It seemed he could not avoid getting her agitated.

"I'm sure it will turn out all right," Martin said, in a soothing voice. "Victoria will settle down eventually, and I'll bet in five years or so you'll have some adorable grandchildren to spoil. I know you would love that."

"Of course I would," she said, smiling. "And don't I deserve it? I would like nothing better than to be a doting grandmother, and to watch my children's children grow up and take a role in the Society of this city. Speaking of marriage and children, Martin, when will we be having this conversation about you?"

Martin sighed again. Now the conversation had veered into the very subject he was afraid to bring up.

"Mother," he said, "I did not think that we would go over this again. . ."

"And why not?" she said. "It is not an unimportant subject, and I do not understand why it is taking you so long to find a suitable girl to marry. You are 44 years old, Martin, and it is past time that you should have found someone."

Should he tell her? This was the reason he had brought her here, but now he was hesitating, unsure, nervous.

He decided to do it.

The waiter came back with their appetizers. Martin was grateful for the interruption, but when the man left he decided to charge ahead with his news.

"Mother, I have found someone."

"You have?" Her eyes lit up, and there were actually were tears at the edges of them. "Oh, Martin, that is wonderful news, something I have prayed for so many times. Tell me about her? Is she someone I know? I do hope she is someone from

Philadelphia, and not from that obnoxious crowd of upstarts in New York. Who are her people?"

Martin cleared his throat. "I do not know much about her people."

"You don't?" Her mother cocked her head, puzzled. "Why not?"

"Because they are from Ireland, and she does not have any contact with them."

"Ireland? Well, perhaps they know your father's cousins Lord and Lady Gordon. They have an estate in the northern part of the country. They are very prominent in the social life over there, and I'm sure everyone knows them."

"I'm sure they wouldn't know the Gordons," Martin said.

"Oh. Well, perhaps they are from a different part of the country. Let's see, I think your father has met some people from the South, a banker and the owner of a shipping company, if I recall. I don't remember the banker's name, but the shipping man is named Williamson. I don't think he's a peer, but he has a huge estate and scads of money. Would they know him?"

"No, Mother. They would not know anyone like that. They live on a small farm. They have been tenant farmers for many years, although I think they are finally buying the property." He took a sip of his soup, waiting for his mother's reaction.

She had raised a spoonful of caviar to her lips, but she suddenly put it down on the dish with a clatter.

"Did you say 'tenant farmers'?"

"Yes."

"Martin, are you joking?"

"No, Mother, I am not joking.

Her face turned white. "This MUST be some kind of joke, Martin."

"No, it is not." He set his mouth. "The woman I have found, who I would like to spend the rest of my life with, is named Rose Sullivan McCarthy. She worked for our family about 15 years ago. Perhaps you remember her."

His mother's lip quivered, and she seemed to be trying to compose herself. "I do remember her," she said, finally. "She left our employ because she was in a family way. The coachman, as I remember, was the guilty party. Is she not the one?"

"Yes."

"Martin, this is shameful," she hissed. "I will not go into the matter of her social status, but she is a married woman!"

"Her husband left her six years ago," Martin said. "He abandoned her, and cannot be found. She can get a civil divorce based on his abandonment. Her Church will not accept that, but she has for all intents and purposes left that denomination of Christianity. I would like to marry her. I have always loved her, Mother, since the day she first came to work for us."

She looked stricken. "Martin, you can't be serious. You would marry that, that Irish serving girl? You are a Lancaster! You would bring shame on our family if you do such a thing." She gripped the edge of the table, her knuckles white, and leaned forward, trying to keep her voice down. "There are so many other fine women out there, Martin. I have introduced you to all the best society girls in this city, many times over the years. I had always hoped — no, expected — that you would make a match with one of them. There is still time — my cousin James York did not marry until he was almost 50 — you could still give up this foolish idea and find someone more suitable."

"No," Martin said. "I have never been interested in the girls you have found for me. Girls is what they all are: silly, shallow girls, nothing more. They talk only of the narrow confines of their life in society. They know nothing of the real world. Why, New York is like a foreign country to them! I have nothing in common with people like that. Rose is a real woman, Mother, and she has lived through more in her time on Earth than a dozen of those silly girls you want me to marry."

The waiter came back with their food, and his mother maintained a frosty silence while the man took their appetizers away and set out their entrees.

"Can I get anything else for you?" he said.

"No, thank you," Martin said, and the man left them.

All of a sudden, his mother's face seemed to fall apart, and her voice cracked. "Martin, this is so heartbreaking," she said. "I have been so disappointed in Victoria, and after everything that happened to young Tom," her lip quivered again, and she seemed about to weep.

Martin put his hand on hers, and said, "Mother, we are all heartbroken that Tom was taken from us at such a young age."

"He was only 15," she said, her voice cracking. "When he got sick and died, I thought the world had ended. I have thought of him every day these last ten years. He would have been 25 this year, and probably married to a girl from one of Philadelphia's finest families. I had such hope for him, and all of you. You are my last hope, Martin." She squeezed his hand, and for a moment Martin thought she would soften toward him.

But then her eyes hardened, and she drew her hand away. "Your father will not be well disposed toward this news," she said coldly. "In fact, I am quite sure he will disown you. Not only that, but you will lose your position with the law firm. The firm will not want to have an employee who will bring scandal to it. You should think about that before you proceed any further with this plan, Martin."

"I have thought about it," Martin said. "I would not like to lose my family or my livelihood over this, but I am sure about my feelings toward Rose."

"A serving girl!" his mother hissed, anger flashing from her eyes. "A common serving girl who could not keep her hands off the coachman. I am ashamed of you, Martin, and I will not feel sorry for you if your father refuses to ever see you again."

Martin felt anger rising in him, but he wrestled with himself to get control. He wiped his mouth with a napkin, very carefully and slowly, and then pushed his chair back from the table and got up.

"Mother, I am sorry this had to happen," he said. "I do not see any reason to continue this conversation, because I am reluctant to say things that will hurt you. I will come to see Father tonight, and we will have a private conversation. If he handles my news badly I expect that our relationship will suffer irreparable damage. For that I am deeply sorry, but I will not change my mind. Goodbye, Mother."

CHAPTER SEVEN

June 1908

"Isn't it a glorious day for an outing at the zoo, my darlings?" James said. It was a Sunday afternoon and he was strolling among the gardens and caged animals of the Philadelphia Zoological Gardens. There was Edith, in a violet high waisted ankle-length dress and carrying a yellow parasol, her wide brimmed hat trimmed in peacock feathers. Six year old Mercy in her bright yellow pinafore, her black hair in ringlets about her face, held her father's hand, while Edith held the hand of four year old John, resplendent in his white sailor suit and holding a big red lollipop in his other hand.

James could barely contain himself on days like this, when the sun was shining and the air was crisp and clean and crackling with possibility. He felt like he could burst with happiness at the wonder and light and people all around him.

The happiness was a bit forced, he had to admit. There had been some unsteady times in the last few years, it was true. Even now he was not sure if Edith trusted him completely. There was still an edge of suspicion about her, a questioning look in her eyes that he would see at times, as if she was trying to figure out just who this man was who lived with her. It had all come about because of the picture she'd found in his steamer trunk five years ago, the one of Rose and the three boys, taken years before when the boys were but children. It was madness to keep that picture, especially since he'd never told Edith about Rose and his family, but somehow he could not let it go. He had thought it safe because he'd hidden the key to the trunk, but Edith could not resist hunting for the key. You could not put a steamer trunk in front of a woman, he'd found, and expect her not to look in it.

He'd had to think fast when she confronted him, and he came up with a story that Rose was his sister back in Ireland, and the boys were his nephews. He spun a yarn that her whole family had died in a typhus epidemic, and that he kept the picture as a memento of her.

He'd never told Edith much about his past, so at least he didn't have to worry about making the details match. He simply made a family history up out of the air, the words pouring out of him in torrents. It amazed him sometimes how easily he could make up these stories. It was almost scary.

Edith bought the story in the end, although she seemed skeptical. She asked many questions, and James finally had to say, "I don't like to talk about it, my love. The memories are too painful."

She stopped her questioning after that, but things never completely returned to normal. There was a coolness that came between them, and no matter how much James tried to thaw it out with his bluster, it never entirely melted away.

"Daddy, I want to see the lions!" Mercy said, squeezing his hand. "Can we go see them, please?"

"Why surely!" James said. "I believe it's feeding time, so we'll have to go inside the Lion House, where they feed the big cats their supper." He led the way inside a large brick building where a crowd was entering. Inside it was cool and dark, and it had a strong, musty, animal smell. When his eyes adjusted to the dim light James saw the group of cages with lions pacing back and forth, waiting for their dinner. They were magnificent, and he watched in awe as the huge animals padded back and forth in their confined spaces, the muscles in their flanks rippling as they walked, their eyes aglitter as they scanned the crowd for a sign of the attendants who would bring them food.

"Little John doesn't like this place," Edith said, as the little boy clutched at her skirt, terrified of the beasts across the room from him. Just then one of the lions stopped and roared, a throaty, percussive sound that echoed off the tile floors and walls, and the boy screamed in terror.

"James, he's petrified," Edith said, gathering the boy up in her arms. "I must take him out."

"Daddy, can we stay?" Mercy said. "I'm not afraid of the lions. I want to see them eat their dinner."

"We'll be out in a moment, my dear," James said, as Edith bustled away with the screaming John. "We'll just watch these fellows take a bite of their supper."

The clock on the wall said five minutes before 3:00, and it was clearly almost dinner time for the cats. With each moment they were becoming more agitated, pacing faster and faster, baring their teeth and roaring so loud James could feel the vibration in his chest.

There was a crowd gathered by the waist high iron railing close to the cages, and James picked Mercy up in his arms to get a better view over the heads of the people nearby. There was a gap of about 20 feet from the railing to the cages, and even though the lions were behind bars it was a terrifying spectacle to see them this close.

They were directly in front of the largest lion in the room, a huge tawny male with a luxuriant brown mane that fluttered with every step he took. His large teeth gleamed and his tongue licked his lips as he scanned the crowd, looking for his meal.

"Take a gander at him, Mercy," James said. "He's magnificent, isn't he? Why, he could kill us all with one swipe of his paw. He looks at us like we're nothing more to him than a fly on his back. If you got near him he'd kill you without even thinking about it. That's a creature not to be trifled with, my girl."

Then, off to the side, there was a sudden disturbance. Someone had separated from the crowd of onlookers and jumped over the railing. It was a young man of about 20, and he was clearly drunk. He wore a dirty gray shirt and blue woolen pants, and he looked like a workman, unshaven and disheveled. He was roaring at the lion, goading it, and strutting about like a circus performer. He had the crowd's attention and clearly enjoyed it, even though some of the women were screaming for him to get away from the lion. The huge animal stopped its pacing and looked at him, its eyes glittering with scorn. There were iron bars on the cage, but there was a gap between them, and the lion could easily reach a paw out and cuff the man if he got closer.

And he was moving closer. James realized that the young man was daring the lion to take a swipe at him, and he was gradually moving close enough to make that a possibility.

And then he realized something else: the man was his son Tim.

He had not seen Tim in years, although he lived less than five miles from Rose and the boys. He could have just as well been living in Patagonia or some far off country like that, however, because Philadelphia was a city of rigid neighborhood boundaries, and people stayed within them. The Irish of Rose's neighborhood would not think of crossing the boundary into the German neighborhood next door, and the Germans would view the Irish as foreigners with whom they had nothing in common. James knew that by living in a Jewish neighborhood with Edith he had effectively walled himself off from Rose and the boys. For all they knew he was living on the other side of the world.

Although he had not seen Tim in a long time, he knew this was his son. The boy had grown into a lean, wiry man with a shock of black tousled hair and a bluish black stubble on his face. He had a sensitive mouth like Rose, and he had her green eyes, but there was meanness in them, and a harshness about his face that James did not remember. He looked dangerous.

He was clearly drunk, though, strutting about and preening in front of the lion, playing to the audience that was alternately encouraging him and crying out for him not to get too close to the big cat.

"Look at the man!" Mercy said. "He's so brave!"

"No, he's being foolish, my darling," James said. "He's much too close for comfort." They were standing by the railing, in full view of Tim, and James began to sweat. What if Tim saw him? Would he recognize James? Of course, he would know him as Peter Morley, the name he used eight years ago when he was the head of Tim's family.

This was a bad situation, to be sure. James wanted to leave, but he thought any movement would draw attention to himself. Tim was only ten feet away, capering around like a Mummer, bowing to the lion and making faces at it just out of its reach. The lion roared repeatedly, as if it were angry at this jester making fun of it.

For once in his life James wished he were a smaller man. He wanted to blend in with the crowd, to disappear, before Tim saw him. He knew the young man would make a scene, and he did not want to have to deal with it. He could make up some story to explain things to Mercy, but what about Edith? If she came back and saw Tim confronting him, she would know instantly that he had lied about the picture she found. She would know that he had another wife and children, a family who did not know about his new life.

"Look!" Mercy cried. "Look what he's doing, Father."

Tim had picked up a stick and he was poking it through the bars of the cage. The lion tried to swipe at the stick, but each time Tim pulled it away before the lion could touch it. The lion was roaring at Tim in frustration, and the young man responded by roaring back, drawing laughter from the crowd. He kept getting closer to the cage, and James wondered why someone did not stop him. By now the crowd was silent, as Tim courted danger by inching ever closer to the great tawny beast behind the bars. The lion watched him with a fierce concentration, waiting for a chance to swipe its huge paw at the stick again.

Tim was now only five feet from the bars, and he leaned forward and started to poke the lion again. This time the lion reacted with a sudden reflexive movement, swiping at the stick so quickly that it pulled Tim forward for a second, so that his head was clearly in reach of the beast's other paw. The crowd froze in terror, and Tim's eyes widened as he realized he could not move away quick enough to avoid that massive paw.

James did not think, he acted. He put Mercy down, leapt across the railing, and charged across the space toward Tim, barreling into the younger man at full force and knocking him headlong onto the floor just as the lion swiped at him with its razor sharp claws.

The crowd gasped, the lion roared, the echo reverberating in the small room, and in that moment Tim looked at James, next to him on the floor, and recognition dawned in his eyes.

"Hey," he said. "I know you. You're, you're—"

"The man who saved your life," another voice said.

It was Paul. He had grown taller than Tim, and had more of James in his looks, although with Rose's red hair. He pulled James to his feet, then offered a hand to Tim.

"I can't leave you anywhere, can I?" Paul said to his brother. "All I did was go off to get myself a soft pretzel, and look at the trouble you got into. You'll be the death of me yet, brother. I'm sorry for the trouble, Mister. My brother likes to tempt fate, it seems."

"Don't you know who he is?" Tim said. "That's Father."

"What? Don't be silly," Paul said. When he turned to look at James, however, shock and recognition dawned on his face. "Wait, are you. . . it's not possible. . . you look just like him. . . are you Peter Morley?"

"No," James said, looking away. "I'm sorry, I think you have the wrong man."

"Do you deny it?" Tim hissed, anger flashing from his eyes.

James broke out in a sweat again, and felt trapped. He had no idea what he was going to do.

"What's going on?" said a voice behind James. He turned to see a big Irish policeman with a red face and bushy black eyebrows looking at him. "Which one of you idiots was provoking that lion?"

"It was me," Tim said, his chin sticking out. "And what's it to you?"

"Why, it's nothing to me if a fool like you gets eaten by a lion," the policeman said. "I only came over because I'd be afraid you'd give the poor creature indigestion. Scum like you would be bad for a lion's stomach, I'd be thinking."

"I'm sorry for the trouble my brother caused," Paul said. It was clear he was the diplomat in the family. "We'll be going now."

"Yes," the policeman said. "You do that." He had a black billy club in his hand, and he was smacking it against the palm of his other hand. "Before I have to get physical with your idiot brother, you do that. Now get out of here, the lot of you. Go on, get out. And break it up, all of you," he said to the crowd. "The feeders have arrived and it's time to let the cats have their supper. Come on, off with you, the show's over."

The crowd moved off murmuring to itself about what it had just seen, and James moved quickly away from Tim and Paul. When he got to the railing, Mercy said, "Father, I was afraid for you," and put out her arms for him to pick her up.

He picked her up and started out of the lion house with Mercy in his arms, hoping to blend in with the crowd. He couldn't resist turning around for one last look at his boys, and when he did he saw them both staring at him, Paul with puzzlement in his eyes and Tim with a murderous rage in his.

CHAPTER EIGHT

March 1910

"Young man, I hear you Morley boys have a wild streak in you," George Campbell said. "Although I've been told that you're a clever fellow, and you have good ideas. That makes it doubly hard to fire you."

Paul was sitting across a large black mahogany desk, polished to a mirror brightness, from the president of the Duncan Paper Mill. George Campbell had a ruddy face, a clipped sandy mustache, and a burr of steel gray hair. He had piercing blue eyes and a square jaw. He was known as a no-nonsense man who did not suffer fools gladly. In his voice there was still the lilt of his native Scotland, although it was only a hint of the Highland brogue he'd brought over to America when he arrived 40 years earlier.

"I understand the two of you have been up to some mischief," Campbell said. "When I heard what happened I wanted to fire both of you, but Seamus Draper, who is my right hand man in the mill, tells me he believes that your brother Tim was the chief culprit, and that you are not to blame. Besides, he says you're a valuable employee, and a smart one too. Can you tell me why I shouldn't get rid of you as well as that troublemaking brother of yours?"

Paul took a deep breath. He had thought he was being called to Campbell's office to be fired. Now, he saw that there was a chance to save his job. Tim had already been fired; he did not want to have to go home to their mother and tell her both of them had lost their jobs.

"I am sorry for what happened," he said. "My brother Tim is a bit hot-headed sometimes."

"Hot-headed?" Campbell said, bringing his fist down hard on the desk. "Why, he almost killed someone! He attacked a man on the warehouse floor and beat him half to death with a hammer. Then, I'm told you got involved and injured two other men so badly they had to be sent to the hospital with the first fellow. What in God's name were you doing? This is a paper mill, not a boxing arena."

"I apologize, sir," Paul said. "But Tim felt that man was insulting our mother. He does not take insults lightly, you see. I tried to smooth it over, but it got out of hand, I'm afraid. The man made one more comment, and Tim could not hold back any longer."

Campbell ran his hand through his short hair. He was a powerfully built man who seemed confined, sitting at his desk. He seemed to be made for action, and his muscles were straining to be up and about, doing something.

"What kind of an insult?" Campbell growled.

Paul cleared his throat. "It's a touchy subject, sir. It was about Tim's, uh, parentage. This man, whose name is O'Hara, lives near us in West Philadelphia. He has heard rumors, gossip, about my mother, and, well, he was just repeating them. Tim loses his temper easily, and the man was goading him, trying to get him mad. I tried to intervene, but as I said, things got out of control. When this O'Hara's friends jumped in and tried to beat up Tim, I had to defend him. It's something any man would have done, sir."

"I cannot have brawls on my premises," Campbell said. "You Irish are always fighting, and for the life of me I don't know why. You're a bellicose race, it seems!"

"Sir, how would you like it if someone cast aspersions on

your daughter Lucy's morals?" Paul said. It was a bold move to bring up Campbell's pretty daughter, who was sitting at a desk outside the office. She was Campbell's secretary, and she worked on one of the new mechanical typewriters, typing letters for him all day long. Paul knew she was off limits to someone like him, but his heart leaped every time he saw her, and he had found excuses to flirt with her whenever possible. He would have given anything for a kiss from her flowerlike lips.

"What do you mean, bringing my daughter into this discussion?" Campbell said. "And calling her Lucy, no less! You're a brazen young man, using her first name, and suggesting—"

"I only meant that the very mention of something like that would get you angry," Paul said. "And it has already."

Indeed, Campbell's ruddy face was even redder, and his eyes were flashing.

"Do you see?" Paul said. "The way you feel is exactly the way Tim felt when that O'Hara fellow started making his insinuations about our mother. I tried to get him to ignore it, but there's only so much a man can take."

"Humph," Campbell said, swiveling around in his chair and staring out the window at a ship on the river. "I don't know about that. . . well, perhaps you're right. I certainly would have a hard time staying calm if someone. . . uh, I understand you handled yourself very well. Draper tells me those men were mighty banged up."

"I have learned to handle my fists, sir. It's been a consequence of growing up where we do, and having the family history we have."

Campbell steepled his hands in front of his face, looking intently at Paul. "When did you come to work here?" he said.

"Eight years ago," Paul said. "I was 11 years old. Tim was 14."

"Helping your mother, were you?"

"Yes. Our father left us, and we had to find work to help out at home."

"I see you've had a bad hand dealt to you," Campbell said. "Still, it's no excuse for acting like a common Irish barbarian. You'll never get anywhere in this world by using your fists to solve problems. I'm afraid I'll have to let you go, son."

This is it, Paul thought. I might as well take a chance. "May I ask a question?" he said. "Why do you make paper that's suitable only for wrapping fish?"

Campbell's face reddened again. "What are you talking about? We make some of the finest paper in the region. What do you mean?"

"I mean," Paul said, "that this mill is good at making a cheap, low grade product that is acceptable for commercial uses, but not for anything that could be used by office workers. There's a market for paper that you haven't explored."

"Office workers?" Campbell snorted. "Who cares what office workers use? I sell millions of reams of paper to the biggest printing companies in this region, son. There is no market for office paper that can compete with that."

"I understand that," Paul said. "But you're being a little short-sighted, in my opinion. That machine out there," he pointed at the next room, where Lucy's typewriter was clacking away, "it's making big changes in the world. How many letters did you write ten years ago?"

"What? I don't remember. . . I had a male secretary then, and he wrote them out it longhand for me. . . I suppose it wasn't as many. No, it definitely wasn't as many as today."

"Lucy tells me you keep her busy all day long typing out bills, letters, memos — all sorts of documents."

Campbell's eyes narrowed. "See here, you impudent pup, what are you doing talking to my daughter? What business do you have in my office? I won't have a common, Irish laborer talking to my daughter!"

Paul held his hands up. "Seamus Draper sent me up here from time to time, to drop off production reports to you. I was just being sociable talking to your daughter while I was in the office." It was a lie, of course — he had made up every excuse he could find to come up and flirt with Lucy, but he wasn't going to tell her father that.

Campbell harrumphed, as if he didn't believe Paul for a minute, but he seemed more interested in arguing his point for the moment.

"I agree that there seems to be more use for those infernal machines all the time — Lucy tells me I need to hire another typist to keep up with all the work — but I don't see your point. Why would I need to explore another market? I am doing quite well as it is."

"You just answered the question yourself," Paul said. "These typing machines are becoming wildly popular, and some offices have dozens of men and women typing away every day. Lucy tells me the business school she went to is expanding, because there is such a need for young women to handle these typing duties."

Campbell raised his eyebrow at the second hint that Paul had been talking to Lucy, but Paul hurried on. "There is a need for a higher grade of paper for these machines," he said. "Much of the paper that is on the market is of low quality, and it tears easily. The ink in the typewriters smears, the paper gets jammed, and it is very frustrating to the typists."

Campbell slammed his palm down on the desk. "God's breath, I get the feeling you're in here every day talking to my daughter! What gave you the idea—"

"Sir, I am a friendly sort of fellow, and I like to talk to all kinds of people. I find it's the best way to learn things; and I like to keep learning all the time. Getting back to the subject at hand, however, why don't you call Lucy in here and ask her about it? She can tell you the problems she has with the cheap paper she is forced to use."

Campbell's chin jutted out at the brashness of this young man, who was about to be fired for brawling, but who was now giving him advice on how to run his business. However, his Scottish soul could not resist the opportunity to find a new market for his products, and he decided to go along with the boy's gambit until he could determine if there was any merit in it.

"Lucy!" he bellowed. Immediately the typewriter stopped clacking, and Lucy appeared at his door.

"Yes father?" she said, coming over to the desk.

She was beautiful, Paul thought once again. She had full lips and silky blonde hair swept back from her forehead and piled on top of her head, and it gave her a regal appearance that was belied by her mischievous green eyes. She also had the hint of her father's square jaw and pug nose; Paul could see that clearly with her standing so close to him.

He felt like grabbing her right here in front of her father and kissing her full on the lips, and he was dangerously close to doing it. The difference between me and Tim, he thought, is that I have enough sense to keep myself from doing things like that, while he doesn't.

"Lucy, this impertinent young man is telling me that there is a need for a higher quality of paper to use in those typing machines. Is that true?"

"I've been telling you that very thing for months now," Lucy said. "The paper we use is no good. We've tried different grades, but it's either so thin that it tears easily, or it's too thick and coarse and jams up the machines. Don't you remember me telling you?"

"No," Campbell said. "I'm a busy man and I have a lot of things on my mind. I don't remember every little detail—"

"Well, I am surprised, Father," Lucy said, her chin sticking out just a bit. "I am not some silly little girl, you know. Paul is only repeating what I told him recently, and it's something I've been telling you for quite some time now. Why are you suddenly paying attention because a man happened to mention it to you?"

Campbell reddened, and started to bluster. "See here, Lucy, I meant to do some thinking about what you told me, but confound it, I just did not have the time. And what do you mean, talking to the likes of this Paul fellow? These boys from the mill are not to be standing around talking to my daughter. Why, if your mother hears this she'll have a conniption."

"Father, I'm surprised at you," Lucy said, putting her hands on her hips. "Bringing Mother into this discussion. This has nothing to do with Paul Morley talking to me, and even if it did, I am old enough to make my own decisions about whom I wish to talk to. I have an idea that could help your business, and it happens that Paul agrees with me. If you would stop thundering for a moment maybe you would learn something."

Paul fell in love with her at that moment, when her eyes were flashing and her chin was jutting out, and she looked ready to face down a tiger. She was magnificent, and he wanted more than ever to kiss those full lips.

"Humph," Campbell said, making a show of shuffling papers on his desk, but clearly on the retreat. "I don't know why I even try to argue with you, young lady. I get more back talk from you than the workers I have to deal with down on the docks. Well, I suppose I should consider this idea of yours. You say there's a need for a better grade of paper?"

"Every girl in my class at business school went to work for an office like this," Lucy said. "In fact, most of them work at larger offices. They all use typewriters and they turn out reams of typing every day. When we get together for Sunday outings, they all complain about the quality of the paper they have to use. There is a market out there for you to exploit, if you're bold about it."

"A market you say?" Campbell said, brushing his fingers across his mustache thoughtfully.

"A promising market," Paul interjected. "All it would take is some research, to find out how to make the right kind of paper for these machines. You would need to buy a different type of wood, and maybe change the manufacturing process a bit. I am sure we could do it."

"We?" Campbell said, raising an eyebrow. "Isn't that a bit forward of you? I was on the verge of firing you, and now you're telling me what 'we' should do. That's a bit bold, isn't it?"

"It may be, sir," Paul said, "but I promise you that you won't regret it. And I'll make it easy for you: I'll take complete charge of researching this new product for Duncan Paper. You won't have to worry about a thing. I'll find out how to make it, and everything we need to do to start selling it. Trust me."

Campbell looked at him skeptically. "And what am I supposed to do, pay you while you're out learning how to make paper? I already have a successful paper mill here, and I don't see why I have to have someone on my payroll who's not contributing his share of the daily workload."

"Oh, Father, give him a chance," Lucy said. "It's not going to cost you very much money, and it's a chance for you to develop a new market. Why, I think it's a good business decision to let a smart young man like Paul take charge of this."

Paul's heart quickened to hear Lucy talk about him like that in front of her father. The air felt electric in the room, and for the briefest instant he saw Lucy's eyes flash with a fierce longing that thrilled him.

Campbell eyed them both. "I suppose it could work. Okay, I'll give you one month to get to the bottom of this, young man. You can remain in my employ, but I want results. If you don't have any in a month, I'll do what I should have done earlier, and fire you."

"I'll need two months," Paul said. "Because I might have to travel out of the state to do my research. Your competitors in town would be too suspicious if I showed up and started asking questions. I will have to pose as a buyer of paper goods, and get my information that way. I'll need an expense account, to cover my travel costs. And there's one other thing."

"And what would that be?" Campbell said, shaking his head. "As if you haven't asked for enough already! Great blazes, boy, but you're a cheeky one. I've half a mind to fire you now for your impertinence. An expense account!"

"Now, Father, you know he's right," Lucy said. "How else is he going to get the money to do the job right? I'm sure he hasn't saved enough from the pittance you pay him to travel around and research this project!"

"All right, but what's the other thing he's asking for?" Campbell said, running his hand through his hair in exasperation. "Next thing, he'll be asking for a share of the profits!"

"I'll need my brother Tim hired back," Paul said. "He needs a job, and since I'll need an assistant, I'd like him hired again."

"That scoundrel?" Campbell said. "Never! I can't have a ruffian like that working for me!"

"Father, please?" Lucy said. "I'm sure Paul will promise that his brother will cause no more problems. Isn't that right, Paul?"

"Absolutely," Paul said. "I can promise you that you'll have nothing to worry about from Tim."

Campbell sighed. "I must be crazy, but I see a bit of my younger self in you, Paul Morley. All right, you have two months, and you'll get a modest expense account, and you can tell your brother Tim he's hired again. But if you can't give me a good report at the end of two months, you and your brother will be out on your ears."

"You won't regret this, sir," Paul said, standing up and shaking Campbell's hand. "I promise you'll be very happy you made this decision." He turned to Lucy. "And Miss Campbell, I will need to meet with you later today to find out more about the ideal qualities of typing paper. Can we discuss this over lunch?"

"That would be very nice," Lucy said. "I would be happy to do that."

Campbell started to redden again, but there was something that made him hold his tongue. He seemed to admire the pluck of this young man. "Get out of here, the two of you," he said, gruffly, "before I change my mind."

Paul left the office with his heart leaping in his chest.

CHAPTER NINE

October 1912

"Mother, my friend Alice says her father saw our father in a motion picture," Mercy said. "Why can't we go to the theater and see him too?"

"Because motion picture theaters cater to a low class of people," Edith said. "We don't go to places like that."

"Then why does Father appear in those picture shows?" John said. "And why are we going to see him at the studio?"

They were riding on a train headed to West Norriton, twenty miles outside of Philadelphia. It was a crisp fall day and Edith had taken the children out of school for this outing.

"Father appears in the shows because he makes some extra money that way," Edith said. "He's been a driver for Mr. Lubin, the owner of the studio, for years now and he just slowly got into the performing end of it. He doesn't appear in those low comedies and men's films that Mr. Lubin makes. You know he has a good singing voice, and Mr. Lubin is trying to create motion pictures with your father singing on them. He has tried many experiments, and he hopes to perfect the technique, so that his moving pictures will some day have sound."

"Won't Father be surprised that we came to see him!" Mercy said.

"Yes," Edith said. "It will be a great surprise for his birthday."

Edith looked out at the passing landscape, the rolling farms just outside the city, and thought about how James had told her what a wondrous place the new Lubin studio, called Betzwood, really was.

"It's a marvel," he said. "Mr. Lubin bought 500 acres and he's built almost a whole city there. It has offices, a boiler house, a plant to process the film, buildings to store the scenery, and a grand big house where the visiting actors live. Why, he even has an all-glass studio for day shots, and two studios without windows for indoor shooting. There is so much electric lighting he can make it brighter than daytime in there! It has all the latest equipment for making motion pictures, and it's bustling with activity every day. There are actors and actresses everywhere, rehearsing their lines, singing, working out comic gags — why, you'd think you were backstage at the Orpheum Theater. It's a grand place, Edith, and I love working there. Mr. Lubin says that he wants to feature me in a film soon. Won't that be a capital thing?"

Edith knew that James was a man with a weakness for looking at himself in mirrors, and she saw how he swelled with pride when he talked of how he might have a career in motion pictures. He had been working on the fringes of this new industry for ten years now, first as a driver for Siegmund Lubin, the immigrant manufacturing wizard who had developed the camera and the studios and started making his own motion pictures ten years ago. Gradually, James had learned other jobs, making himself useful in various ways for Lubin, even to the point of appearing in marginal roles in some of Lubin's short films. When Lubin heard James' voice, however, he began talking of making a short film of James singing and synching it to a wax cylinder recording. It took a while to work out the technical details, but James had said that things were moving along smoothly now, and it would not be long before they had something ready for theatrical release.

She worried about this new chapter in his life, because she

was not sure if she could trust him. It had been ten years since she found the picture of the woman and three boys in his steamer trunk, and even though he swore passionately that they were not another family, they were simply his dead relatives from Ireland, she never completely believed him. She saw how women responded to him, how they looked at him, and how he enjoyed the attention, and she could not be sure what he was doing, especially now that he was surrounded by theater people. He was a big man with a shock of black hair that had turned gray around the temples, giving him a dignified air, and he had a smile that could light up a room.

"It will be so much fun to see Father," Mercy said.

"Yes, because he's never around," John said, wrinkling his brow, his hands clenched into fists in his lap. "He's always working at that studio."

"He's just trying to make money so we can have nice things," Mercy said. "You know he would like to see us more, but he can't."

Edith marveled at how the children could see things so differently. James was Mercy's hero, and she would not ever hear a bad word said against him. Little John hungered for his father's attention, and was resentful that he did not get enough of it.

It was a strange thing, she thought, that James could be such a hearty, good-humored man around other people, but yet he was sometimes prone to silences and dark moods around his family. He would cut himself off from Edith and John, but the only person he seemed to relax and open his heart to completely was Mercy.

The train pulled into the station and Edith and the children got off. There was a black Model T Ford car parked near the platform with a sign that said, "Taxi For Hire" on it. A skinny boy wearing overalls was leaning against it, chewing on a blade of grass. He looked barely sixteen, but since no one else was around Edith realized he was the taxi driver.

"Can you take us to the Betzwood Studios?" Edith said.

"The movie place?" the boy said. "Sure can, ma'am. Are you an actress? I've driven some famous theater people there, like Harry Myers, Ethel Clayton, Arthur Johnson, even a pudgy young fellow called Oliver Hardy who I just know will be famous some day."

"Our father is James Francis," Mercy said. "He's a famous singer."

"Never heard of him," the boy said, holding the door for them.

"He's not famous," Edith said, settling into the back seat. "Just a worker at the studio, I'm afraid. We're his family."

The boy went around to the front of the car and cranked it, then jumped in the driver's seat when the motor caught, making a terrible racket, and he put the car in gear and it lurched forward. It bumped noisily along the rocky dirt roads at a snail's pace, and Edith wondered again if these new inventions like motor cars were really making life better. The world seemed a lot more peaceful when you could clop along at a measured pace in a carriage pulled by a horse.

"Like I said, I've driven all sorts of famous people here," the taxi driver said, shouting over his shoulder to Edith. "Say, but some of those actresses are pretty!"

"I am sure they are," Edith said.

"People say they have loose morals, though," the boy said. "Of course, I wouldn't know about that. I just drive them, you understand. I don't have much more to do with them than that. But I reckon Show People are different than you or I; they live by different rules."

"Yes, I suppose so," Edith said. She suddenly had a bad feeling about this visit. Was it a mistake to show up at

Betzwood unannounced? Should she have told James she was coming? What if she caught him doing something wrong?

But why shouldn't she surprise him on his birthday? He turned 50 years old today, and wasn't that a perfect reason for his wife and children to surprise him? Why should she have this feeling of dread, that she was going to catch him doing something wrong? After all, they had been married eleven years now; wasn't that enough time to be able to trust her husband?

"There it is," the boy said, coming over a small hill and pointing to the vista before them. There were green fields stretching out on both sides of the road, and off to the right there was a long driveway that led to a cluster of buildings on the top of a rise. There was smoke coming from the boiler house, Edith could see lots of people and activity, and she could hear someone's voice shouting orders from a bullhorn.

"Look, Mother," Mercy said. "They're having a battle!"

Sure enough, there was a group of what looked like Indians on horseback charging a small hill that had a contingent of blue coated soldiers who had dismounted and were firing back at them. The air was thick with gray smoke from the rifles, and there was the popping sound of guns being fired.

John was wide-eyed, gripping the back of the driver's seat, his body taut with excitement. "Is that what Father does?" he said. "What a bully game they're playing!"

"They're shooting another Western," the driver said, turning down the long driveway. "They shoot several pictures at once, you know. They're probably shooting a different picture right now in one of the studios."

"I can't wait to see what Father is doing!" Mercy said. "Do you think he is one of the soldiers over there?"

"He could be anywhere," the driver said. "They use folks wherever they need them. It doesn't have to be a professional actor or actress. If Mr. Lubin needs an extra person for a scene, he'll grab anybody. He put me in one of his pictures once — I had a bit part in a production called 'A Trip To Mars'. He got sued for that one. He's been sued by Thomas Edison, and lots of other folks. They say he copies their pictures, but he don't care — he just keeps turning out more pictures all the time."

He brought the car to a noisy halt in front of the main building, a palatial stone house that looked like something a country baron would live in. It was three stories high with white columns, an ornate carved wood front door, manicured gardens, and a view of a crystal chandelier inside the first story windows. Next to it was a brick two story office building that was bustling with activity. There were people in costumes milling about, men carrying clipboards shouting orders, burly men in work clothes carrying props and sets, actors sitting in chairs waiting for their next call, and everywhere the sense of urgency, of Time moving at a furious clip.

Edith was at a loss for what to do, and for a moment she thought, maybe I should not have come. The driver seemed to sense her hesitancy, though, and he said, "Ma'am, I would start by going inside that building. The main office is in there, and they can direct you where you want to go."

"Thank you," Edith said. She paid him his fare and ushered the children inside the building. Just inside the door there was a desk with a bespectacled young man at it.

"Can I help you?" the young man said. "Are you here for a job?" He looked very businesslike, with a high starched collar and a brown woolen suit on. He had a thick brown mustache that covered his mouth completely.

"No," Edith said. "My husband works here. We came to visit him."

"What's his name?" the man said.

"James Francis," Mercy said, proudly. "He's a singer."

"Did you say he's your husband?" the man said to Edith. He seemed to turn a bit pale under his mustache. "Is that what you said?"

I should not have come, Edith thought. Something is wrong here.

"Yes," she said. "He is my husband. Do you know where he is?"

"Well, uh, he's probably next door in the studio. I think they're shooting right now, though. He probably can't be disturbed. Yes, I'm pretty sure he can't be disturbed."

"Next door?" Edith said. "The building right over there?"

"Yes," the man said. "But, as I said they're shooting, and he can't be — wait, where are you going?"

Edith marched the children with her out the door and through the crowd of people to the building next door, then she went straight in the door and made her way down a long hallway, following the sounds of people talking.

With each step her heart beat harder, and she became convinced she was going to find something bad happening. There was a door at the end of the hall but she pushed through it, a woman on a mission.

She forgot that she had her children with her, forgot that she had come to surprise James on his birthday, forgot everything besides the rage building up inside her. At the end of the hall there was a closed black painted wooden door with a sign on it that said, "Studio 3". She heard laughter coming from inside and she pushed open the door.

At first she could not make sense of what she saw. There were many people standing around in costumes, and there were huge cameras and lights everywhere, blinding her for a few seconds.

There were men in gray military uniforms and women in fancy gowns, and the room was decorated to look like a ballroom, with a chandelier hanging from the ceiling and a five-piece orchestra playing off to the side. It looked like a debutante ball or cotillion, and everyone in the room had the look of Old Money.

Even James, who was standing in a crisp gray uniform near the bar across the room, laughing as if he'd just heard the most hilarious piece of gossip.

He had his arm around a blonde girl, and she was laughing just as hard. She had a full skirted cream colored gown with a bustle and lace sleeves, and her hair was done up in ringlets like a Southern belle of forty years before. Edith realized this was some type of film about the Civil War, and James must have been playing a Southern officer. He was wearing a fancy uniform with gold braid and buttons, a red sash, and an ornate scabbard for the sword at his side.

"Is that Father?" John said. "Why does he have his arm around that woman?"

Edith had forgotten that the children were with her. She had been consumed with such a burning desire to find James that she was almost in another world. John's comment brought her back to her senses.

"He's, uh, just playing a role," Edith said. "I'm sure it's just a role in one of Mr. Lubin's moving pictures."

"What are you doing here?" a man said, coming up to them. "This is a closed set, Madam. We are getting ready to shoot a scene and visitors are not allowed."

Edith struggled to figure out what was going on in front of her eyes. "You mean you are not shooting this minute?" she said.

"Of course not," the man said. "They haven't started the next scene yet. The actors are taking a break, but we will be shooting again in five minutes."

"They are not acting?" Edith said. James was still unaware

of her presence, and now he began playfully kissing the blonde girl on the neck, and she giggled and pretended to push him away.

"What is Father doing?" Mercy said, her eyes wide with shock. Then, she bolted across the room and ran straight to him and put her arms around his waist, burying her head in his chest. James looked stunned to see her, and the blonde girl pushed herself away from him in embarrassment. The girl looked up to see Edith marching toward her, and then turned and beat a hasty retreat.

"What a surprise," James said, lifting Mercy up by her shoulders. "My favorite people in all the world have come to visit me!" He looked shaken, and he was obviously trying to pull himself together and think up an explanation for Edith, who was now standing in front of him, with John in tow.

"We came to surprise you for your birthday," Mercy said, leaning back to look at him, her eyes aglitter with hurt. "What are you doing with that woman, Father?"

"Oh her?" James said. "Why, that's Helen LaCouer, my dear. She's a famous actress. I am playing a scene with her in Mr. Lubin's latest, ah, drama. It's about the War Between The States, don't you know. I have my biggest part yet. I'm sure it will be a very popular picture show!"

"Why are you hardly ever home?" John said, his arms crossed in front of his chest. "I never see you anymore."

"Why, ah, I am busy at the studio, you know," James said. His face was flushed, and he was sweating. "This place is a regular hive of activity, and there are several picture shows being produced here every day. Mr. Lubin keeps me busy doing all sorts of jobs — and now I'm appearing in the shows, with the other actors."

"You are a liar, James Francis," Edith hissed. "I am sorry I brought the children here to see your shenanigans. You are not a man to be trusted, I am afraid."

"Now, Edith, I can explain," James said. He looked distressed, his brow knotted in worry.

"NO," Mercy said, pushing him away. She scrambled out of his arms, then kicked him in the shins. "You are not my father," she said, tears streaming down her face. "I hate you!"

James looked shattered. He held his arms out to her, pleading. "You don't understand, my girl. You just don't understand. It's nothing serious. All just a bit of play acting. A child's game, really. Don't you understand?"

"Are they bothering you, James?" It was the man who had asked Edith what she was doing earlier. He was some type of assistant, and he looked like he wanted to escort Edith and the children off the set.

"No," James said. "No, not at all. Why, I'm happy to see them."

"We will not bother you anymore," Edith said, in measured tones. "We are leaving. Come, children. We will leave your father to his play acting."

She took their hands and walked out, leaving James looking like a man washed up on shore who realizes for the first time that he is shipwrecked.

CHAPTER TEN

September 1, 1916

James walked along Market Street in the twilight like a ghost, seeming insubstantial and almost so thin that he did not cast a shadow. People pushed past him on their way to get to the train station, and he staggered each time, as though the smallest force could make him lose his balance.

He did not have an appetite anymore, and his body looked like it. His clothes hung on him loosely and his once handsome face was gaunt and haggard. He was unshaven and his white-gray hair was tangled.

He was out for a last walk in the city, just wandering about for an hour or two before it was time to go back to his room and kill himself.

He had decided to hang himself in his room, because it seemed the only thing left to do. He would have been hanged all those years ago for killing that Lieutenant Charlesworth, and now it seemed a fitting thing to finish the job, to put the noose around his neck that the British Government would have wanted to do for him in the 1880s.

It was only what he deserved, was it not?

He stood at the corner of Market and Broad streets, watching the crowds of people bustling everywhere, the street throbbing with energy and the noise of the cars, buses and trucks everywhere you looked.

Where were the horses? For a moment, it was as if he were transported back in time to when he first came here, fresh off the boat from Ireland, and he remembered the sight of all the horses pulling carriages, carts, wagons and trolleys, all clopping along bobbing their heads in time to the pace of their hooves on the cobblestoned streets. They were magnificent animals, brown and black and tan, some with white marks on their noses, all of them with muscles rippling from the effort of pulling their loads. There was a smell, such a strong earthy smell, of horse in the air!

Now, they were gone, all except for a few poor hucksters and draymen who couldn't afford a truck to drive their wares about. They were replaced by noisy, unpredictable, automobiles careening everywhere, stinking of gasoline, their horns a cacophony of screeches and yowls, frequently colliding with each other and scaring pedestrians out of their wits. Everyone was in a hurry now, there was such a frenzy to get places fast, and the measured pace that James remembered from his youth was gone.

The past was fading away, disappearing by the hour, and no one seemed to care. James used to like that things changed so fast in this country, but now it was all speeding up, the future crowding out the past at a furious pace, murdering everything that smelled of yesterday.

He looked at the fading light slicing through the tall buildings all around him. He had had hope once, and he remembered the way it carried him, lifted him like a wave and how he had believed anything was possible in this crazy sunrise country, this place of beginnings.

Why, he had appeared in a motion picture show! He had been right at the center of the world of moving pictures, playing roles with real actors and actresses in Mr. Lubin's pictures. His face had been on a poster or two, and he had thought it was all finally going to come true, his dream of being a someone, something special and real to make up for the nothing he was as a boy back in Ireland.

But it was not to be. Two weeks ago the Lubin Manufacturing Company had closed its doors. The magnificent studios at Betzwood would never more see the bright light, the colors, the sounds of moviemaking. It was all gone, gone forever.

The fire in 1914 had started the decline. It had been a disaster, destroying sets, equipment, and negatives at the company's studio in Philadelphia. The negative of James' biggest role to date, of a romantic lead in a comedy, was utterly destroyed.

As if that wasn't bad enough, the Great War that was raging in France meant that Lubin lost his European market.

The death blow came weeks ago, when after years of litigation against Lubin by Thomas Edison, the courts had decided in favor of the old man from Menlo Park. Edison had patents on just about every technical aspect of moviemaking, and he had used the courts to intimidate his rivals and force them to do business with him or lose their markets.

Lubin had held out as long as he could, but when the end came it was swift. "We're shutting down," he said. "I'm not selling enough of my films to pay my expenses." He was angry, defiant. "I'll be back, don't you worry about that. I'll figure this out. I'll have the studios back in business in no time."

But James knew the time had passed. The fire, Edison, the war, changing tastes — it had all combined to bring Lubin down with amazing speed.

"What are you waiting for? Get going!" the big policeman who was directing traffic yelled at James, and he shuffled along across the intersection. He was 54 years old and out of a job — Lubin couldn't afford a new suit of clothes these days, let alone a driver — and he did not know how he would find work. Some of Lubin's actors and production workers had already moved to California, where new companies were setting up shop to make pictures, and James had thought about moving. In the end, he'd been afraid, though.

He didn't have the confidence. The last few years had been one setback after another, and they had combined to make James feel like he had been beaten up, chewed up and spit out by this beast called Progress.

Why, I don't even have a family anymore, he thought as he reached the other side of the street. Edith had kicked him out three years ago, and in spite of his pleading with her to take him back, she had said no. She had a lot of English grit, and she wasn't going to change her mind, it seemed. It broke his heart not to see his children, especially little Mercy, who seemed to hate him now.

I've made a mess of everything, it seems.

And how old were his boys with Rose now? Why, Tim would be 28 years old, and Paul 25, and even little Willy was a full grown man of 22! He hadn't seen them in years, and he wondered what they looked like now.

And Rose. . . what would she be doing now? He had not set eyes on her in 16 years. He remembered kissing her on that moonlit night back in Skibbereen so many years ago. Who knew where their paths would lead? If he could go back there and change things he would, but it was like trying to stop the flow of a great river, impossible.

You couldn't hold it back no matter how hard you tried.

Each time you did or said something it sent ripples through the stream, and each one of those ripples affected other people, changing their lives in ways you never could have predicted.

And the ripples kept expanding outward, kept expanding endlessly, affecting people far removed from you, the echoes continuing infinitely.

Which is why he had decided to hang himself, because he

could not stand the thought of how many lives he had damaged, could not carry the weight of the past any longer.

He wandered along the street, not knowing or caring where he was headed, simply enjoying his last hour of existence before he headed back to his room.

He came to the corner of 6th and Market streets, near to the Carpenter's Hall, the historic building where the U.S. Constitution was signed, and he saw a crowd out in front of the building. There were large arc lights on poles giving the glare of daytime to the scene, there was a band playing patriotic songs, there was a speaker's platform, and someone was shouting to the audience. It was then that James noticed signs posted everywhere, saying, "America's Duty To Come To The Aid Of Her Friend Great Britain — A Presentation By Major John Charlesworth."

He felt as if he'd been struck in the stomach, and he gasped for air. Charlesworth? That was the name of the officer he'd killed in Ireland. It couldn't be the same man, that was impossible. Still, how many British officers named Charlesworth could there be?

He made his way through the crowds of people, elbowing them aside as he got closer to the platform.

There were a number of official looking men seated on the platform, some wearing military uniforms, but James couldn't see all of them because the speaker's podium blocked part of his view. There was a man at the podium, a politician of some sort, waving his arms and talking about the threat to civilization posed by the German Army, and how America needed to step up and join this fight to save the world from domination by the Hun. He talked of the great bond between the American and British peoples, and after five more minutes' worth of histrionics and fist thumping that brought applause from the crowd, he proclaimed that the next speaker was, "A

British officer fresh from the trenches at Verdun, who will tell us of the great need our cousins have for a helping hand from us. I give you Major John Charlesworth!"

A man in his mid-30s, with a clipped auburn mustache and blue eyes, wearing an olive drab tunic, green tie, and tan jodhpurs with brown boots, strode to the podium. His jacket was covered in medals and regimental patches, and he stood with military precision, his back ramrod straight, as he looked out at the crowd.

James was stunned. The man looked exactly like the Lieutenant Charlesworth he had beaten to death more than 30 years before. How could this be? He tried to make sense of what he was seeing, and finally, he realized when the man opened his mouth and a different voice came out, that this was the son of the man he had killed. Where the father's voice had been laced with contempt and sarcasm, this man's voice was gentler, kinder, more measured.

He spoke of the conditions on the Western Front with a great sadness, talking of the thousands of young men who were dying every week, 19,000 British dead in one day alone at the Battle of the Somme, how this terrible trench warfare with the German Army was destroying the flower of British and French youth, how the world would never be the same again, and that America needed to come to the aid of its European cousins so that the stalemate would be broken and the war ended before thousands more died.

He was interrupted at times by cheers, but there were also some catcalls. "We don't need to get involved in Europe's wars!" one man said. "Settle it yourselves," said another. "We will not sacrifice our boys to settle the Old World's fights!"

The Major answered them all with a measured calm, never getting upset or emotional. He was the soul of British propriety, asking for help but never begging for it, using reason to overcome emotion.

When he finished there was polite applause, and he went to take his seat on the platform. James stood there and listened to several more long-winded speeches, determined to wait them out.

When the last speaker had thumped his fist one more time and the band played their last patriotic song, the crowd started to disperse. James, however, sidled over to the platform and waited for the Major to come down the three steps on the side. When he did there were several people waiting to talk to him, so James stood off to the side and let them have their say. When the last ones, a group of teenaged boys anxious to join the war, had finished and walked away James saw his chance.

"Major Charlesworth," he said. "I believe I knew your father many years ago." It was a reckless thing to say, and James shuddered with fear as he said it.

The Major raised his eyebrows. "You did? Well, I must admit I don't encounter many people these days who knew my father. Did you serve with him?"

"No," James said. "I, ah, well, I knew him when he was posted to the barracks outside of Tullamore, in Ireland." It was like someone else was talking, and James was listening to his own voice turning traitor on him.

"Good God, man," Charlesworth said. "That is where he died. Can you possibly spare a few moments? I would love to talk to you about this."

"Why, certainly," James said. He was manic with a crazed glee now, with the thrill and terror of walking on the edge of a sheer cliff. He did not know what would come out of his mouth next, and his heart was pounding from the excitement.

"Do you know a place where we can talk?" Charlesworth said. "A local pub, perhaps?"

James led him down the street to a place called "Jim

Maguire's", a watering hole favored by local politicians and businessmen, where he had been with Siegmund Lubin more than a few times. They found a quiet table in the back, and James used some of the few dollars he had left to order a round of beer. Charlesworth wanted to pay, probably because James looked so down on his luck, but James would not let him.

The Major lost no time. "What do you know about my father?" he said, as soon as the waiter had brought them their steins of beer.

"I know he was in that battle in South Africa. What was it called — Isandlwana?"

"Yes. He distinguished himself there. He received several decorations for bravery under fire. He was a man of great courage, I am told. I was only two years old when he died, so I don't have any memories of him."

"I see." James realized that Charlesworth had been living with an image of his father that he had created out of stories told to him by others.

"And that is why I am eager to know any details about him," Charlesworth said. "Now, tell me — how did you know him?"

"I worked in the stable of the barracks," James said. "Just a stable boy, you see." How much can I tell him? he thought. I am talking to the son of a man I killed. What if he suspects me? Can I still be hanged for what I did?

Despite his fear, James was on the verge of telling him, of unburdening his conscience. It had weighed on him for so long, and he wanted to be over it, no matter what the consequences. He shifted in his chair, preparing himself.

"A stable boy?" Charlesworth said, his face falling. "Then you would not have worked with him very closely. I always enjoy talking to men who served with him."

He looked so disappointed that James decided to embellish.

"Ah, but I saw him almost every day. He looked a grand figure astride a horse, I can tell you that. The man was majestic, the way he mastered those animals!"

Charlesworth looked pleased. "Yes, I have heard he was a great horseman."

"Oh, to be sure. He had that air of command. It was the same with the men. I know his men would do anything for him. The way they snapped to it when he gave them an order! He was a born leader, your father."

"Yes," Charlesworth said. "It is true, he was born for the military. His father had a distinguished career, as did his uncle. They both made general. I am sure my father would have gone on to have just as great a career if he had not been cruelly cut down by those Irish rebels."

James blinked, not understanding. "Irish rebels?" he said. "Is that what you said?"

"Yes. You did not know that? Didn't you say you lived near the barracks?" Charlesworth eyed him suspiciously.

James struggled for an answer. "Well, yes, but I left for America when I was still a young man. . . I haven't been back in all these years, you see. . . I did not know whatever became of your father. You say he was killed by Irish rebels?"

"Yes, brutally murdered. They attacked him in his office in the barracks. There was a furious fight and he was killed. The men escaped, but when his sergeant found him my father was still barely alive. He told him the story with his last breaths. He died a hero."

James was thunderstruck, and he could not speak for a moment. It was obvious the Major believed every word of the story, and his eyes shone with pride for his father. The beefy sergeant Billings must have made up the story to cover his own failure to protect his superior officer.

All these years this man had believed a falsehood about his

father's death. It was astounding. Should I tell him? James thought. He desperately wanted to unburden himself, to release his guilt about his terrible crime, but how could he tell the man's son that his father had not died a hero? That he had died from a blow to the head from a boy, a dirt-poor Irish boy who had lashed out in reaction to the sneering contempt of a British officer? A boy who should have been crushed under Lieutenant Charlesworth's boot heel, not standing in triumph over his fallen body like David did against Goliath.

He could not do it.

"Yes," James said, finally. "It seems your father died a hero. It sounds like the man I remember."

"Do you know anything more about him?" the Major said, leaning forward in his chair. "I would love to hear more about him, since I know so little."

"I am sorry," James said, pushing his chair back and standing up. "I do not know anything more. I was simply a stable boy, and I only saw him from afar. I wish I could tell you more, but I can't. And now I have to go, Major Charlesworth. It was a pleasure meeting you."

"Yes, it was good to talk to you," Charlesworth said, looking disappointed. "I thank you for the conversation. I am always happy to talk about my father."

Out on the street, James decided that he wanted to live, for his children. He realized that he would live on through them, and he wanted them to have a picture of him like the one Major Charlesworth carried in his mind of his own father. James could not bear to have them remember him as the false, unreliable, deceitful man he had been.

He looked at the crush of humanity around him and decided he would live. Maybe I can send some ripples through the stream that will make things turn out differently, he thought.

CHAPTER ELEVEN

July 4, 1918

    Mother,

I am writing to you from the field hospital at Abbeville, in France. I don't know if you have received a letter yet from the War Department, but I wanted to let you know that Tim and I are all right. We were both injured in battles along the Matz River several weeks ago, and we ended up in the same hospital here.

    I am the better of the two. I received some minor flesh wounds, which got infected and caused some concern, but the infection is gone now and I am healing well. I am up and about, and I visit Tim every day.

    Tim has had a hard time of it. There was a furious artillery bombardment when the Germans started their offensive, and Tim was on the front lines, where he saw and heard some fearsome things. A lot of his comrades fell that day, and although he was not wounded physically he saw things he will never forget.

    If that were all it would be simply a case of dealing with nightmares for the rest of his life. However, on June 11 he was gassed during the French counter-attack, and he almost died. Thank God, he got his gas mask on before he got the worst of the fumes. Still, he has received permanent damage to his lungs, and he was blind for a time. Luckily the blindness went away, but his eyes have been weakened and that will not get better, the doctors say.

    Tim is being sent home later this month. I am sure you will receive more details about it soon, and you can make plans to meet him at the train station in Philadelphia. You will have to be patient with him, Mother, because he is not the same Tim you remember. His bravado is gone, and his nerves are very bad. He cannot stand too much light and movement, and he tires easily. I think you will have a challenge to keep him away from the whiskey, because he asks for a drink constantly (although the doctors do not give him any).

I wish I could come home and help you with him, but the Army is sending me back to the front in two weeks. I helped to rally the troops during the heaviest fighting along the Matz, and I disabled some German machine gun emplacements that were taking a heavy toll on our boys, and for my actions I have been promoted to lieutenant. I am told that officers are needed for a big push that is planned. The word is that the war is going well for the Allies, and that the Huns are in retreat. With so many American boys coming over each week we have the advantage of numbers, and the French want to press that advantage and try for a quick end to the conflict. With any luck we'll have this thing ended before Christmas. I promise you I will do my best to avoid further injury.

I know this letter must be distressing to you, Mother, and I am sorry to have to send it. I know you did not want Tim and I to enlist last November, but when Tim came to me and said he wanted so badly to do it, I could not argue with him. His life has not turned out well so far, and I think he was hoping for some way to distinguish himself. I know that sounds crazy, to go off to war in the hopes of making something of yourself, but perhaps it is not such a crazy thing to do. Tim was looking to change his luck, I suppose, some grand gesture that would redeem him from the life of frustration and disappointment he has known for so many years.

Although I am Tim's younger brother I have always felt that I needed to look out for him. You know that he has been an angry person for most of his life, but especially since our Father left us. I have gotten in many fights over the years in order to help Tim out of the scrapes he has gotten himself into. I think he saw the Army as a way to channel that rage, to use it in an arena where he would be *praised for it.*

If so, he was right, because he was doing well as a soldier. He had several commendations for bravery, and he rescued a wounded man at Arras in March under heavy German fire. He was beginning to find his way, although this is a terrible place to find it in. War is not like anything else in life, and the people who do well in war are not suited for normal life ever again. Even if Tim had come back unharmed in body, I do not know whether he could have gone back to his old life. We have all seen too much.

I hope that I can manage a normal life myself, after what I have been through these past six months. I have seen enough bloodshed to last me a lifetime, and I want nothing more than to come home, get married, and settle down to a quiet life.

I am going to ask Lucy Campbell to marry me. Running across open ground under a rain of German shells has a way of focusing a man's mind, and I have decided I cannot live without Lucy, and I want her to be my wife. I am doing well at her father's paper company, and even though, as you say, I am of a different social class than the Campbells, I will ask her father for her hand in marriage as soon as I get back to Philadelphia.

I know you do not approve. When I brought Lucy to meet you, I saw the look in your eyes. You think she is a spoiled rich girl who looks down on people like us. I know she was raised in different circumstances, and I admit her mother is a bit haughty, but I have hope that we can overcome those outdated ideas about class. We live in America, after all, a country that is supposed to be free of those confining categories. Thirty years ago when you worked for the Lancasters perhaps there was an insurmountable wall between the classes, but nowadays it is being torn down. Believe me, Mother, I have seen men from all classes shot in this war, and they all die the same way. Men still call out for their God and their mother when they are dying, no matter where they went to school or how much money they have.

Lucy's father is a blunt, no-nonsense sort of fellow and he made it clear at first that he was not happy about my interest in his daughter. That was years ago, however, and nowadays he is better disposed towards me. I have proven myself a capable man in his company, and my ideas have helped to develop new markets for his products. He has promoted me several times, and I know he thinks I am an asset to the firm.

I have tried hard to improve myself. I read constantly, to make up for my lack of schooling, and I try to learn new words and use them in my conversation. I want to make something of myself, to be a proper husband for Lucy.

Mrs. Campbell does not see me that way, unfortunately. It is clear that she does not like me, and I am sure she would rather that Lucy found a different beau. When I have called at the Campbells' home for Lucy she treats me with a frosty silence, and Lucy says there have been arguments at home over my interest in her. I will do my best to win her over, but regardless of whether or not she likes me, I am determined to marry her daughter.

I know you will think me foolish for doing such a thing, but I am so in love with Lucy that I would risk everything, even her parents' disapproval and the loss of my job, to marry her. I hope you understand. Wasn't that the way you felt when you married Father? I know it was many years ago, and things did not turn out well, but if you remember the flame you carried in your heart back then, you will understand why I am determined to do this. Whatever the future brings, I will not regret this decision.

I do worry sometimes that I have too much of Father's unpredictability in my character. I can be reckless at times, although I have more prudence than Tim. I am afraid that I could be led astray by my passions, and hurt people the way that Father has hurt us. It is for that reason that I have never tried to find Father, even though I have heard of his whereabouts from time to time. I know, for instance, that he was working as a chauffeur for a man named Siegmund Lubin, who made moving pictures in a studio outside of Philadelphia. I did not tell Tim this, because I was afraid he would go there and do harm to Father, and I suspected I was capable of the same acts myself. I am much like Tim, as I said, except that I am able to master myself better than him.

What makes us like that? Is it something about our Irish nature? Father never told us much about where he came from in Ireland, but when this war is over I would like to stop in Ireland and try to find out. I know your family is from Skibbereen, in West Cork, and I will visit there also, and find the family farm. You told us so many stories about your childhood, and all those stories your mother had about the Good People, and I am fascinated to see with my own eyes the land of my forebears.

Ireland has had its portion of suffering, of course, and we must pray that things turn out right in that troubled land. There is much talk over here among the British soldiers about the Irish independence movement, and some feel it is ungrateful that the Irish refuse to be conscripted into service to help Britain in its time of need. The Irish want to throw off the yoke of British rule and be a free and independent nation, and who would blame them? It is July 4, after all, when we Americans celebrate our independence, and I can only hope that Ireland will win the same freedom that we have enjoyed for 140 years. Independence never comes without a cost, however, and I fear that when the war is over there will be hard feelings on both sides, and more bloodshed.

There has to be more than this crazy world of suffering, there has to be more for us than simply to live our lives hurting and killing each other. Seeing this war up close has convinced me of that. And do you know what is astonishing to me? That both sides in this war call themselves Christians. I have seen dead German soldiers with a crucifix around their necks; those same men were trying only minutes before to kill me and my comrades. They were sent into battle with the prayers of their priests to aid them in the most complete and total *destruction of their enemies.*

Maybe your mother was right and there is another world of happiness and magic all around us, if we but had eyes to see it. Maybe your mother was not mad; it could be that she simply had the ability to see a better world than this.

Perhaps I will get a glimpse of it in Ireland.

I must go soon. Please give my love to Willy. I am sorry that he is so sickly with consumption, but maybe that is for the best, since it prevented him from fighting in this terrible war. I feel better that he has been home with you, so that you are not alone. Please give my regards to Mr. Lancaster. He has been very kind to our family, and I am glad that he has been such a good friend to you. I do not know what may have happened to us years ago when Father left, if not for the kindness of Martin Lancaster.

I hope that the war will end soon. Maybe I will be home to see you by Christmas. I will do my best to come home in one piece. Please pray for me.

Once again, please be patient with Tim when he comes home. He will need all of the patience and love you can give him, for I fear his life will be even more troubled than it was.

Your son,

Paul

CHAPTER TWELVE

December 24, 1918

"Have you ever seen such a glorious night, Lieutenant Morley?"

"It's something special, Agnes," Paul said.

He was standing on the deck of the SS Olympic, looking out at the mid-Atlantic ocean which was as smooth as glass, the cloudless sky above spangled with a billion stars. Next to him was Agnes O'Hare, the nurse who had saved his life two months before. He had come down with the deadly Spanish flu in October and had spent two weeks in a hospital in France in the grip of delirium, his body racked with bone-rattling coughs, his lungs filled with fluid and his breath coming in shallow gasps. Thousands of soldiers had died from the illness, and the hospital was overflowing with patients. Agnes was a Red Cross nurse who took an interest in him, and she spent nights putting cold compresses on his fevered head, giving him water, changing his sheets when they became drenched with his sweat, and holding his hand when he cried out in terror at the visions he was seeing.

He hovered between two worlds for many days, and he saw many strange visions and heard voices. There was an old Irish woman in a black shawl who stood by his bedside and talked of a land of music and dancing, of kings and queens who held court in the forest glades, and of fierce battles, terrifying creatures and beautiful maidens.

The old white-haired woman held out her hand to him,

beckoning, and he almost took it. It would have been so easy to go with her to the radiant land that echoed with laughter, and he wanted to, but something was holding him back. He tried hard to remember, and sometimes he heard the name, "Lucy", but he could not match a face with the name.

Then there was a hand holding his, and a voice telling him to hold on. He gripped the hand fiercely, and when his head cleared he saw that it was a nurse, her brown eyes set off by the white nurse's cap, her smile like a beacon in a stormy sea. She was calling him back to life, and he swam toward her, knowing that he must try to get back to shore.

The crisis passed and he recovered, slowly feeling his strength come back, although he remained weak for a long time, and even now he tired easily and felt his breath come short when he exerted himself too much.

He was grateful to the nurse, but he was also uncomfortable around her. She had shared an intimacy with him, sitting by his side while he cried out at the visions he was seeing, and he felt naked in front of her now. He had been weak and helpless all those nights when he was sick, and it made him feel vulnerable.

He would remember embarrassing moments, like once when he was sleeping and he woke up to find her sitting next to the bed holding his hand and stroking his hair. For a time he simply laid there and smiled up at her, enjoying the feeling of her closeness after so many months in the male world of guns and death. Then, he remembered Lucy, and he pulled his hand away.

He had gone to thank her on the day he left the hospital. She was standing by a window crying and when he asked why, she said, "Haven't you heard? The war is over. The Germans have signed an armistice."

He did not understand why she was crying, but he felt the

need to hold her, and so he put his arms around her. She melted into his arms and put her head on his shoulder. He had not been this close to a woman in many months, and he stroked her hair and told her everything would be all right. She raised her head and for a moment it seemed they would kiss, but then he broke from her and said, "I have to go. I have a train to catch back to headquarters," and he left.

He thought about her all the way back to headquarters on the train, but when he arrived the first thing that Major Peterson said was: "God is good, Morley. We're going home," and he did not think about her after that.

Now here it was two months later, and Agnes had found him. She had come up to him on the second day at sea and said hello, and they had spent many hours together since then. She was going back to Chicago, to her job as a bookkeeper, and she said it would be hard to go back to the quiet life after the things she had seen. "We have all been wounded, and we need time to heal," she said.

Now it was Christmas Eve, and they had taken a stroll on the deck on an evening of uncommon jewel like brilliance and clarity. Paul felt a bond between them, and it had been so long since he had felt the softness of a woman's presence that he could not resist her touch, her closeness, her receptivity. She drew him out, asked him questions, got him talking about his life, and he simply let himself go, surprised to hear some of the words coming out of his mouth.

"So, you say you visited Ireland since I last saw you?" she said.

"Yes," he said. He pulled a packet of cigarettes from his breast pocket, and held them out to her. She took one, and she waited as he lit a match and held it to the end of her cigarette and then his own, before extinguishing the flame.

He took a drag on his cigarette, then exhaled and said: "I

told my mother I would go back to see her birthplace before I came home. I took a ship from France to Queenstown, Ireland, and I made my way back to the farm she grew up on."

"What was it like to go back to your mother's home?" she said.

He sighed. "It was not at all what I expected. I had a picture in my head that was very different than the reality. My mother had told us stories, you see, and the stories did not prepare me for what I saw."

"What did you see?" Agnes said.

He sighed, looking out at the calm sea. "I saw a tiny sliver of rocky land with a miserable little stream running through it, not the big rolling fields I had imagined. I saw people whose hard life had turned their hearts cold and stony. I have an aunt Theresa who inherited the farm, but she is alone and bitter. Her sister Annie moved away to Liverpool and her brother Brian died in the Easter Rising in 1916, when the rebels he was in league with tried to take over Dublin and proclaim the independence of the Irish State. He was shot or blown up by a British shell; no one knows how he died."

"Wasn't your aunt glad to see you?" Agnes said. She took a drag of her cigarette, and the end of it glowed orange in the night.

"No. She closed the door on me when I told her who I was. She came back outside when I started to walk down the lane, but she never warmed up to me. She is an old woman now, and she never married. She lives alone on the farm, and hires men to help her. She has a lot of bitterness about how her life turned out. She thinks my mother got the best of things, emigrating to America. She has spent her life imagining how wonderful things are in America, and my mother, on the other hand, always made us feel like Ireland was the best, most magical place on Earth.

"We all spend our lives living in the future or the past," Agnes said. "Never the present."

Paul took a drag on his cigarette, and exhaled, laughing. "Yes, the only time people really live in the present is during a battle, I think. Being fired at is wonderful for focusing the mind. Time stops and you can feel the eternity of every moment when you realize it could all end in the next instant."

Agnes looked out at the sea. "You're right. The problem is that most of us don't ever realize that until it's too late. I saw a lot of men die in the last year, and they were all outraged that it was ending so soon. They would have given anything for another minute."

Their eyes met, and something passed between them, and with a wordless cry they were in each other's arms, their cigarettes thrown over the side like miniature shooting stars arcing toward the sea.

Paul pressed Agnes against the rail and kissed her wildly, passionately. His lips had hungered for this, and they got their fill, kissing her on the neck, the cheek, the eyelids, the hair. He was like a man possessed, and he lost all thought of himself; he wanted only to slake his hunger, to forget everything about war in the arms of a woman. Agnes moaned in ecstasy, in the throes of a hunger equally as intense, and she pressed her body to him. He felt the hot flush on her skin, heard the pounding of her heart that matched the pounding of his own heart in his chest. He ran his fingers through her hair, then to the hollow between her neck and shoulder, and he thrilled to the touch of her smooth skin. He rained kisses on her, murmuring words of love, and she answered in kind, pulling him to her like a drowning woman.

He wanted to take her there, against the railing, with the billion stars above them and the eternity of glassy sea stretching out before them. It was like what he felt on the battlefield: there was only the Now, no future or past, nothing but Now. All his senses were keen, he could hear the hum of the engines below them, the laughter of officers in the bar two decks below, the whooshing sound of the ship cutting through the waves, the sleepy conversation of two sailors fifty yards away. He could smell the salt air, the lilac-scented perfume she wore, the cigarettes. He could see all parts of the ship, the stars, the endless ocean. He sensed it all at once, and he knew the only reality was this moment and he must capture it now, take her now, take every bit of potential from this moment and make it real.

And then he had a vision of Lucy, standing on the dock when his ship pulled away ten months ago, her eyes filled with tears, her hair blowing across her face, and suddenly he was pulled back into the flow of Time. The moment vanished, the Now was gone, and he had a past and a future again.

He grabbed Agnes by the shoulders and pushed away.

"No," he said, panting, trying to clear his head. "No, I cannot do this. I am sorry, but I must go."

She grabbed his arms and held fast. "No. I need you, Paul. Please stay."

He was sorely tempted. He could feel his body wanting to do it, and he felt poised on the edge of a great cliff, ready to jump.

No. It was just the thing that Tim would do, jumping into the inky blackness without a second thought. He did not have that luxury. He had to be the responsible one. There was no one else; Tim was damaged and Willy was too weak. It had to be him, Paul.

"I need to go," he said. "Goodbye." He turned and walked away, and never looked back.

CHAPTER THIRTEEN

January 2, 1920

"Are you nervous, Rose?" Martin said. They were walking up the steps of the Federal Courthouse building in Philadelphia, and Rose was bundled up in a navy blue woolen coat, her white hair peeking out from the black bell-shaped cloche hat Martin had bought her as a Christmas present. "You need a proper outfit for your big day," he'd said when he gave it to her. "It's not every day you become an American citizen."

Rose had resisted the idea of becoming a citizen for so many years, mostly because she always held out hope that she would someday return to Ireland. When Paul came back from the Great War the year before, he sat at her kitchen table and shattered that hope.

"You have no home there, Mother," he'd said. "I don't mean to sound cruel, but there is nothing left for you. Your brother is dead and your sister Annie has moved to England. The only one left on the farm is your sister Theresa, and she has no interest in you. She spent the duration of my visit complaining about how everyone abandoned her. She is old before her time, and she does nothing but complain about how hard her life is. She is talking of selling the farm and moving to a rooming house in Skibbereen."

"It has been so long since I've seen her," Rose said. "I thought she would tell you stories from our childhood. Did she have nothing good to say?"

Paul hesitated, then said, "No. She said you brought shame on the family because of. . . well, you know."

Thirty years fell away in an instant, and Rose felt the shame come over her again, the shame that made her want to curl up in a ball and lie in bed when she read the letter from Theresa all those years ago with her father's angry words about how she got pregnant without being married.

This time, however, she did not curl up. She slammed her palm down on the kitchen table and said, "I will not let the past rule me anymore. I am done with it."

It was that moment when she decided to get her citizenship papers. There was no more dreaming about going back to Ireland. I have been in this country for forty years, she thought. It is past time I became a citizen here.

She took a class for people preparing for naturalization, sitting among all the new immigrants, people from Italy and Eastern Europe, the latest wave of people seeking a better life here, and she studied about citizenship in the United States of America, the laws of the country and its history.

Now it was time. Martin had picked her up this morning in his ancient Model T, all he could afford on the limited salary he made defending petty criminals who usually had no money to pay for his legal advice. He was dressed in his best suit and tie, and he had his brown Chesterfield coat and bowler hat on, and although they looked a bit frayed and worse for wear, he beamed with such pride when he looked at her that Rose saw nothing else but his smile.

He parked the car on the street near the courthouse, and escorted her up the steps. They were ushered into a room that had dozens of people in it, their faces alive with excitement at what was ahead. Martin and Rose sat near the coal stove in the corner and warmed themselves, and Martin held her hand while they waited. Rose had already taken her written tests and got a perfect score. Now it was time to take the Oath of Allegiance.

Then a large wooden door opened and a clerk led them down a hallway and to a courtroom. Rose had never been in a courtroom before, and she marveled at the carved wooden bench and the high windows and the white marble statue of the goddess Justice blindly holding her scales. There were inscriptions on the walls in Latin, and Martin read them for her in a hushed whisper. She was thrilled to be here, and she felt as reverent and awe-stricken as if she were in church.

Finally another door opened and a judge strode in wearing his black robes. He was a white haired man with a square jaw, and he was the picture of dignity. Every conversation stopped immediately, and all eyes turned to him. He did not waste any time; he made them all stand up at once and after giving a little speech about how they were receiving the privilege of American citizenship and they must take it seriously and make sure to vote in every election, he administered the oath. As Rose repeated the words, she saw tears in Martin's eyes, and deep, abiding love. This is my home after all, she thought, and he is the man for me.

They decided to go out to lunch to celebrate afterward, and Martin took Rose to a restaurant he knew near City Hall, called Jim Donovan's. It was a roomy place with a black and white tiled floor, and long mirrors on the wall, a place where white shirted waiters with black vests scurried about carrying trays of chicken, veal and steak, and the oyster stew it was famous for. It was more expensive than Martin could afford, but he wanted to celebrate Rose's new citizenship.

In front of the restaurant there was a newsboy hawking the day's newspaper, which had headlines about the coming of Prohibition. "Read all about it!" he shouted. "Only two weeks till it's illegal to buy alcohol!"

"What will Tim do?" Martin said, after they were seated. "I don't think he can live without whiskey."

"I don't know," Rose said, "but he is on his own now. He left me yesterday, on New Year's Day. He said that since Paul got married two weeks ago, he could not bear to live with Willy and me. He is closer to Paul than anyone in the world. I don't know what will become of him. The gas attack he suffered ruined his lungs, and he has a cough that will not go away. He cannot keep a job because he is sick so much. On top of that, he drinks more than ever."

The waiter asked if they would like to order a drink. People everywhere seemed to be obsessed with alcohol, as if they wanted to get their fill of strong drink before it was taken away when Prohibition started in two weeks.

Martin ordered a glass of wine, but Rose had nothing. She rarely drank alcohol, since she had seen it ruin too many lives among her countrymen.

"When the Eighteenth Amendment becomes law it will probably mean more business for me," Martin said, after the waiter had brought them their food. "There will be people who flout the law by making and selling their own liquor, and they will be caught. Then they'll have to hire lawyers like me to defend them. I think it's foolish for the government to try to legislate liquor out of existence, and it won't work. People will break the law rather than give up their whiskey."

"I'm afraid that's what will happen to Tim," Rose said. "He can't live without it, and it will bring him trouble. He has fallen in with a bad crowd of men who like to drink as much as he does. He loafs about at the barber shop in our neighborhood, and it's a place with a back room where they play cards and drink and bet on horse races. People say they've already put the word out that they'll be selling homemade whiskey there in a few weeks."

"He had better watch out," Martin said. "The police will be on to places like that."

"Things just never seem to go right for him," Rose said.

"It is true he has had a lot of bad luck," Martin said, "but God will watch over him, I am sure."

"You have more faith than I do," Rose said, with a shrug. "I struggle to believe sometimes. I do not know why we suffer so on this Earth, why we have to say goodbye to people and places who mean so much to us, why love is such a losing proposition."

Martin smiled. "Rose, Rose, you have the Irish perspective on this. I do not believe it's all heartache and sadness. Of course, my people did not have the anguished history yours did. Still, you have much to be happy about. Your Paul just got married, did he not? And she seems like a fine young lady."

"As my mother used to say, 'Och'", Rose said, shaking her head. "There's no good will come of that, Martin. I told Paul many times I thought he should not marry that girl, but he would not listen. She is too far above his station. Why, her mother would not come to the wedding! It was a hasty, thrown-together thing, as you well know, all because they got married without her mother's approval. The woman thinks my Paul is not good enough for her daughter. No good comes of mixing the social classes."

Martin broke out into a laugh.

"And what's so funny?" Rose said.

"Listen to you," Martin said. "You sound exactly like my own mother, when I told her I wanted to marry you. She said those exact words, Rose, and so did my father, before he banished me from the family. I didn't know you had so much in common with my parents."

"Well, it's true," Rose said. "It hasn't done you any good to know me, Martin Lancaster, and that's why I won't marry you.

If you hadn't met me you'd be a lawyer working for a fancy Philadelphia firm, and you'd have a big house on the Main Line and belong to the Union League where you'd meet all your rich friends for lunch. Instead, you've been driven out from your family, and you can barely make ends meet defending thieves and other petty criminals. Why, you don't even have an office! You have to make do with a chair in the courthouse waiting room."

"Yes, but I am happy," Martin said. "Happier than I would have been working in some stuffy law firm and going out to lunch with the boring fellows I went to school with. I find my clients to be infinitely more interesting than the corporate liars and swindlers I'd be defending if I'd stayed in that other world. The only thing that would make me happier is if you'd marry me, Rose Sullivan Morley."

Rose felt herself blush. "Why, it's indecent, the idea of me, a woman almost 60 years old, getting married. You should act your age, Martin Lancaster."

"No, I refuse to," Martin said. "That's the beauty of the life I lead now. I have learned that the world I lived in was stuffy and stagnant, and it was making me old before my time. The people I deal with now get in trouble because they take too many chances, because they're always looking for a big score around the corner, and you know what? It's taught me something. I'm not saying I want to be exactly like them — they don't have the best judgment and they certainly make a lot of mistakes — but, by God, Rose, they are optimists. They have hope and faith — things don't always work out for them, but they keep trying."

"You've been around criminals too long, Martin," Rose said, laughing. "It's addled your brain."

Martin chuckled. "No, it's made me see things clearly. I want to marry you, Rose, and I'm going to ask you once again, right now."

He got down on his knees next to her. He pulled a wad of brown paper out of his pocket, and unwrapped it to reveal a tiny gold ring. "Rose Sullivan, love of my life, will you marry me?"

Rose put her hand to her mouth. "Martin," she whispered. "We're in the middle of a restaurant! You can't do this here!"

"Why not?" Martin said, laughing. "Here is as good a place as any. I repeat: Rose Sullivan Morley," and this time he said it loud enough for the whole restaurant to hear, "Will you take my hand in marriage?"

CHAPTER FOURTEEN

June 1922

James did not know where they were taking him, but he was afraid he was going to be meeting people he did not want to meet.

He was sitting in the leather back seat of an expensive automobile, blindfolded and with a throbbing headache. The headache was from the blow he had received from the butt of a pistol an hour before when he had refused to go with the strange men who had knocked on the door of his room.

"We need you to come with us," one of them, a short man with a wide brimmed hat had said. "Somebody wants to talk to you."

"What's this about?" James said. It was 9:00 at night and he had been in the middle of writing yet another letter to Edith pleading with her to take him back when there was a rap at the door.

"You'll find out," the short man said. "Just come with us."

"I don't go places with men who show up at this hour," James said, starting to close the door. "Come back in the morning and maybe I'll talk to you."

The short man's associate, a taller man with the wiry build of a middleweight boxer, pulled a gun out of his pocket and hit James on the forehead with the butt of it, and it happened so quickly James could not avoid the blow. His head exploded in pain and he crumpled to the floor. He vaguely remembered being helped down the steps and into the back seat of a car, then blindfolded, but the details were fuzzy and he had spent the better part of the past hour trying to figure out where they were going and why.

He knew they were outside the city and passing through a rural area, because the road had gotten very bumpy, and he could smell manure from the farms they were passing. The men spoke in grunts and hushed whispers, and he knew this was a bad business he was involved in.

It's my own fault, he told himself. I knew what could happen if I started making poteen and selling it.

But what other choice did he have? He was a man of 60, his body in pain from arthritis, and no one wanted to hire him. It was not like the old days, when he had been a coachman. Back then wealthy people couldn't be bothered with dealing with sweaty, smelly horses and their balkiness, their need for food and water and rest. Now, everybody had an automobile, and most of them wanted to drive the machines themselves. The few rich people who still had drivers didn't want an old, broken-down one like James Francis. He had been living in a room by himself, barely surviving, when Prohibition started, and immediately he saw that he could use his old skill at making spirits, learned at Murphy's knee so many years ago in Ircland, to make a few dollars.

That was all he really wanted, was a few dollars. He thought he could sell small quantities of what he made, just enough so that he could pay his bills, and maybe send Edith some money once in a while. He still wanted to be part of her life, and of his children with her. Mercy, his darling girl, was now 21 and engaged to be married. James wanted badly to give her a good wedding, to pay for a grand ceremony with all the trimmings, and he thought he could do that with the profit from his poteen.

He built a still in an abandoned warehouse down by the

river, and it was there that he made his poteen. He used potatoes, sugar and yeast, but it was not the ingredients that made the best spirits, as Murphy used to say, it was the timing. You had to know exactly how much time to spend on each part of the process. There was no science to it, though — it was an intuition, a hunch, that if you got it right gave the drink its bite, the warm feeling going down and the little kick at the end.

He had planned to keep it a small operation, but Americans had a powerful thirst for strong drink when it was suddenly unavailable to them, and he quickly had more work than he could handle. A stream of unsavory characters kept showing up at his room with wads of cash, and demands for more product. The word was spreading that this old Irishman could make a drink that people liked more than the crude bathtub gin that was available in the back rooms and speakeasies.

That was why he was sitting here blindfolded in the back of a car. James knew he was being taken to meet someone who wanted to make a deal with him. Someone who wanted to corner the market on his product. He figured they would offer him more money as an inducement. There would also be the other part, where they told him what he could expect if he did not cooperate with them. It would not be pleasant, he knew.

The car finally turned off the road and onto what seemed like a driveway. It was rutted so bad the car was bumping up and down furiously. The smell of manure was even stronger now, and James assumed they were on a long driveway leading to a farm house.

When they finally stopped the men got him out and marched him across a yard and up three steps and inside a door. They pushed him down in a chair and ripped off the blindfold, causing him to wince in pain at the bright light from a kerosene lamp that was next to him on a table.

When his eyes adjusted he realized he was in a kitchen. It

had a green, chipped linoleum floor, a black cast iron stove and sink, an ancient white icebox in a corner, and a heavy wooden table and chairs, where he was sitting. The two men stood near him but did not sit down.

"He's here," the short man said, standing at the doorway that led into the rest of the house.

In a moment there was the sound of footsteps in the wooden hallway, and then a man came into the room.

He was a white haired man in a tailored black pinstriped suit, carrying a gold handled cane and wearing several gold rings on his fingers. He looked like a bank manager, except that he had an ugly three inch scar across his cheek. He sat down across from James, reached in his pocket, and pulled out a cigar.

"Care for a smoke?" he said, holding it out to James.

James shook his head no.

"Suit yourself," the man said. He put the cigar in his mouth and waited while the short man lit it, then exhaled a puff of smoke and smiled. "There's nothing like a good Havana cigar, I always say."

"Why did you bring me here?" James said.

"Getting right down to business, are we?" the man said. "Good, I like a man who doesn't waste time. I don't suppose you remember me, do you?"

James stared at him closely. He looked vaguely familiar, but James couldn't place him.

"I used to frequent a saloon where you sang on Saturday nights," the man said. "You have quite the voice, boyo. It brought a tear to my eye, hearing you sing 'The Rose Of Tralee'. I believe you were known as Peter Morley then, weren't you?"

"I don't know what you mean," James said. "My name is James Francis."

The white-haired man let out a laugh, opening his mouth

wide enough that James could see a row of gold fillings. "Faith, boys, we've got a comedian on our hands," he said, turning to the other two men. They laughed mirthlessly, showing their teeth.

The white-haired man said, "Ah, that was beautiful. I enjoy a good laugh. It helps the digestion, they say. However, we must get back to business. I understand you've fallen on hard times, Peter."

"I told you, my name is James Francis."

In a flash the man had his hand on James's throat, and he was choking him. His grip was like an iron collar around James' neck with the thumb pressed against his airway. James put both hands on the other man's strong fingers, trying to pry them free, but the man was too strong. It was like trying to open a locked door without the key. He spluttered and squirmed in his chair, but it was no use.

"Now, it would be a good notion for you to listen to me," the man said. He had his face up close to James, and he was speaking in a whisper. His eyes were a slate blue color, like the Delaware River in winter. "For you see, I'm not a man to be trifled with, lad. I like to be told the truth, and I have little patience with liars. You, my fellow, have no allegiance to the truth, that's plain to see. You'll have to change that attitude if we're going to do business together. And do business together we will, whether you like it or not."

He released his grip, and James fell back against the chair, choking and retching, his lungs burning with the effort to get the air they so desperately needed. He had to fight the impulse to take a swing at the man. Calm down, James, he told himself. There's three of them and one of you, and you'd have no chance.

The man sat back in his chair and took another puff of his cigar, then blew the smoke meditatively. "Perhaps we're starting off all wrong, lad. Let me introduce myself. My name is Aloysius Declan O'Toole. Born in Dublin, but emigrated to America in the year of 18 and 95. The short man over there is Seamus Corgan. His friend is known as Blackjack Malone, and I'll leave it to you to work out how he got that nickname. Pleased to meet you."

He held out his hand, but James did not take it.

"I'm sorry you feel that way," O'Toole said, withdrawing his hand. "I'm not a violent man, despite what you may think. I've had an education, you know. Why, I went to Belvedere College in Dublin only a few years before James Joyce. You've read Joyce?"

James shook his head no.

"A pity," O'Toole said. "He's beginning to make a name for himself. He's a fine writer, a credit to our race, although this new book of his, 'Ulysses' is a muddle. I prefer Yeats, myself. Poetry fits the Irish soul better. You must have an appreciation for language, seeing as how you're such a fine singer."

"Jesus, can't we get to the point?" Corgan said. "All this talk is wasting time."

O'Toole sighed and shook his head, all the while looking at James. "You see what I have to deal with," he said. "Surrounded by Philistines I am. They know nothing of literature or art."

"We have customers," Corgan said. "People are waiting for us to deliver. We can't be wasting time, Aloysius."

"Ah, yes, Time," O'Toole said. "We're all under its tyranny, aren't we? Well, I suppose we must get down to the heart of the matter. I understand you make a brand of moonshine, or poteen, as they called it back in the old country, that is quite the stuff. I don't indulge in alcohol myself, but people tell me what you make is very good. It goes down smooth, they say, and doesn't cause a nasty headache the next day. Is that true?"

James thought about saying no, but he did not want that iron grip around his neck again, so he said, "I've been known to make a bit of poteen, yes."

"Good," O'Toole said. "I'm glad we're finally having a conversation. Now, because I've heard such good things about your concoction, I'd like to make a business proposition to you. My friends and I," here he motioned in the direction of the other two men, "would like to be your partners. We can set you up with everything you need to produce large amounts of that liquor. We'll do it right here, out in the farmlands of Delaware where nobody will notice, and we'll take care of the sales and distribution end of it. All you need to do is make the stuff, and we'll get it out to the customers. You'll get a generous cut of the profits, and you won't ever have to deal with the public, as it were. What do you think, my friend?"

"It's against the law," James said.

O'Toole let out long laugh, his body shaking and tears coming to his eyes. He pulled a red silk handkerchief out of his breast pocket and wiped his eyes with it. "We have a comedian among, us, boys," he said, turning to his associates. "Why, of course it is breaking the law," he said to James. "You'll find no disagreement from me on that point. But, don't we all break the law in our own way?"

"I make less than five gallons of the stuff in a month," James said. "I'm a small operator, and all I do is sell enough to keep me from living on the streets. The police aren't interested in me, but they'd surely take notice if I had a bigger operation."

"A fair point," O'Toole said. "However, I'm an experienced man at dealing with the police. Most of them can be paid off, and the ones who can't, well, there are other ways of dealing with them." He smiled, and James saw the gold teeth again.

"I won't do it," James said. "You can talk all night if you want, but you'll never convince me. I don't want to be thrown in jail at my age. Now, why don't you just take me home and we'll forget about this unpleasant meeting?"

O'Toole drummed his well-manicured fingers on the table. "Let's change the subject for just a bit, shall we? As I said before, I remember you from when you were calling yourself by a different name. You used to sing on Saturday nights at Paddy Boyle's saloon. I was a sort of silent partner in that enterprise. Paddy paid me to keep things nice and quiet." He winked at James. "It's a very noisy thing, you know, to have someone break every piece of furniture and all the glassware in a saloon. Paddy didn't want that kind of noise, so I made sure he got it."

Here the two men let out a guffaw, and O'Toole smiled. "My friends have simple pleasures," he said. "They enjoy breaking things. Anyway, not long ago when my sources told me about you and then pointed you out one day, I said, 'That's Peter Morley from Paddy Boyle's!'. They told me your name was James Francis, but I smelled a rat. I made a few inquiries about you, and I found that you've had an interesting life, boyo. Would you like me to go over it?"

James felt sweat breaking out on his forehead. The air was close in the room, heavy with humidity. There was a flicker of lightning, and then the low rumble of thunder in the distance. His fingers were twitching in his lap, and he wanted to act, to dive across the table and choke O'Toole, to pick up his chair and break it across the heads of the two grinning men standing across from him, to do something rather than just sit here impotently.

Steady James, he told himself. Hold back. You'll only get yourself killed if you try something rash.

"I understand your reluctance to answer me," O'Toole said. "A man who's left his wife and three children and changed his name doesn't really want to talk about that, does he? Why, it's a sore subject, I'd wager. I wonder, do you still go to church, Peter Morley? Does your local priest know the dirty details of your life? Have you gone to confession, my boy?"

"I don't know what you're talking about," James said. "My name is James Francis, not Peter Morley."

"Do you want me to hit him?" the man named Blackjack said. "How about I hit him?"

O'Toole put his hand up to silence him. "You are trying our patience," he said to James. "As you can see, my associates would like to persuade you by physical means. The Jesuits who educated me used to say that the body is but a shell, and there's a kind of spiritual pain that is much more intense than the physical kind. I think we can still get this matter resolved in other ways." He nodded to Corgan. "Bring our friend from the other room in here."

"With pleasure," the short man said. He left the kitchen and went down the hallway. James heard him talking to someone in another room, and then footsteps coming back down the hallway.

"I think you know this associate of ours," O'Toole said. "In fact, I do believe you're related to him."

James turned to see his son Tim standing in the doorway.

"Hello, Father," Tim snarled. "It's been a long time."

James could not speak. It was shocking enough to see Tim here, but it was doubly shocking to see the deterioration in him. He was only in his early 30s, but he looked ten years older. His face was lined and sallow, he had the caved in chest of a consumptive, and he was already going gray around his temples. He had the look of violence about him — his nose had been broken several times and he was missing the index and ring fingers of his right hand.

"Hello, Tim," James managed to say. "How are you?"

"Oh, I could be better," Tim said. "Much better, if you

would listen to what these fellows are proposing. It would be good for me, good for all of us, if you'd stop being a stubborn old fool and do business with them."

"I'm surprised at you, Tim," James said. "What they want to do is against the law. It's not right."

"And since when did 'right' mean that much to you?" Tim sneered. "You've never given a damn about what's right or wrong. Was it right for you to walk out on Mother the way you did? And her with three little children?"

"You don't understand," James said.

"Don't I? Well, maybe I don't. I guess I don't understand how someone could walk away from his family the way you did, only to move across town and start a new family under a new name."

There was such hatred in Tim's face that it stunned James. He saw every mistake he had ever made written across Tim's face, and he knew there was nothing he could do to change that.

"Now, now, gentlemen," O'Toole said. "Let's not fight. Sit down, Tim, and let's talk about this like proper businessmen." He motioned toward a chair on the other end of the table, and Tim went around and sat, all the while keeping his eyes fixed on James.

"I can't stand to look at him," Tim said. "I need a drink just to keep from going over there and choking him to death."

"It's not a bad idea," O'Toole said. "Seamus, get out your flask."

Corgan reached in his back pocket and brought out a small silver flask, handing it over to Tim. Tim quickly unscrewed the cap and took a long drink. His eyes rolled back in his head, and James saw that his body had a powerful need for the drink.

"That's enough," Corgan said, grabbing the flask out of Tim's hand. "You don't need to drink the whole thing."

Tim wiped his mouth and looked back at James. "You have a talent for making liquor, old man. It goes down smooth but has a kick to it. There's lots of people who'll buy this stuff. You need to come to your senses and go into business with Mr. O'Toole."

"Well said, my lad," O'Toole interjected. "Although I'm a strong believer in the wisdom that comes with age, in this case I think the father should listen to the son."

James ignored him. "What are you doing mixed up with these men?" he said, to Tim. "There's no good can come of this."

Tim laughed bitterly. "Do you think I have a choice? The Germans ruined my lungs and took away two fingers in 1918," he said. "And that's made it hard for me to find work. I've gone hungry lots of times, Father. The only thing that saved me was Prohibition. I sell some bootleg whiskey and gin, and I make enough to live on. That's how I met Mr. O'Toole and his friends. What they're proposing would make us all a pretty penny, and for the first time in my life I might actually have enough money to live like a decent human being. You could do this for me, Father. The way I see it, you owe me."

James looked at the ruined face across from him and was filled with remorse at all the damage he'd done in his life. Maybe, just maybe, he could make up for some of those mistakes this one time.

"All right," he said. "I'll do it."

CHAPTER FIFTEEN

May 1925

Rose looked out the window of the train at the way the landscape changed as they got further from the city. The streets crowded with brick houses, churches, and warehouses turned into rolling fields and pastures, dotted with little towns bustling with activity. She wondered again, as she always did when she visited Paul's house, why he had to live so far away from West Philadelphia.

It was Lucy, his wife, who had decided to move all the way to this northeastern suburb of Philadelphia. It was called Cheltenham, after a town in England, and Rose thought that alone made it seem pretentious and snobbish. Why couldn't they have picked an Indian name, like so many other places in Philadelphia? Names like Wyomissing, Tacony, Wissahickon, had the echo of the people who lived here first. To name a place "Cheltenham" made it seem like you were trying to give yourself the odor of Englishness, the patina of respectability. Whenever Rose visited she found the place suffocating, a town built up overnight to look like a 400 year old village, all the houses so self-consciously "quaint" and pretty, with the golf club right on its boundary and the husbands all taking the train into town to their jobs as lawyers and financiers.

Paul had done well for himself, it was true. He was a vice president at Lucy's father's company, all because of his cleverness at developing new products and finding new markets for the company's paper. He was making a good salary, and Lucy was living in the style she was accustomed to.

But money doesn't protect you from disaster, Rose thought. It had only been two months since Paul and Lucy's baby had died. Little Claire, a darling little cherub, only three months old, had died in her crib. Lucy was inconsolable at the funeral, and Rose would never forget the sight of Paul walking down the aisle after the church service carrying the little white coffin, tears streaming down his face. She had not seen him cry like that since he was a little boy, not since the time he realized his father had left and was never, ever coming back.

People leave; that was one thing Rose had learned in her long life. You come together with people and then they leave. This baby had come into their lives for such a short time, had still been at the beginning of her time with them, and then she was gone. Was it harder to lose like that, to say goodbye at the beginning, or to spend years with a person and then have them go?

Rose had lost a child too. It was less than a year since Willy, her youngest boy, had died. He had always been sickly, and Rose had always worried a fever or infection, some wasting disease, would carry him off. It wasn't that at all; he had died playing baseball with some friends at a Fourth of July picnic. He had been hit in the head with a pitched ball and died instantly. When the policeman came to her door she thought it was about Tim, that he had gotten in trouble again. "Baseball?" she had said, shrieking like a banshee. "My son was taken from me because of a boy's game?"

It was insane, unjust, absurd, and she cried out to God in anguish.

Why? Why do you do this to me? What have I done to deserve this pain and suffering? Every time I think that things are finally going well, I get hit again. Why give me a heart if all you do is break it over and over again?

She held her tears in at the funeral. She would not cry in front of Paul and Tim. They had seen too much hardship, and she would not let them see their mother wounded. She had to be strong for them.

She thought somehow that Peter would show up at the service. Years ago she had overheard Paul and Tim talking about him, and she'd gotten the impression that he was still in the area. If so, maybe they would know how to get in touch with him, and they would tell him that his son had died. She would not ask them; the subject of their father was closed, and she would not mention his name around them.

She could not help looking for him at the funeral, though. She peered into the dark corners at the back of the church, wondering if she would see Peter's tall frame standing silently in the shadows. He was not there.

"You had a hard life, my son," she whispered to Willy as his casket was lowered into the ground, on the rainy, gray day in November. "You will not miss it."

Martin was with her, and he held her hand as they walked across the rocky ground of the cemetery and he held her fast in bed that night as she sobbed and wailed and cried out that she wished she could have died instead of Willy. Martin was always there, like an anchor, and she held on to him with a fierceness born of desperation.

She let the tears out that first night, but then she was finished. There was no sense in crying over and over about a heartache. Lord, if she did that she'd never be able to live, for heartaches came all the time.

And that's what she aimed to tell Lucy, she decided, as the train wheezed to a stop at the Cheltenham station. She picked up her bag and made her way out of the car and onto the platform. Paul, who was waiting for her, had asked for her help. He had come to see her yesterday at her job in the lady's dress department at Wanamaker's and had said, "I don't know what's the matter with Lucy. Losing the baby has made her different. I think she's cracking up, Mother. I've never seen her like this."

His face was sallow and lined, and he looked scared. Rose did not like her daughter-in-law, but she knew Lucy was the love of Paul's life, and it would shatter him if anything happened to her. I will not lose him too, she thought, not after all the other losses I've had. No, I will do whatever it takes to help him.

She strode right in to the office and asked for a week's vacation from her supervisor, and although old Miss Hallam frowned and clucked that it was highly irregular not to give more notice, she finally tossed her head and allowed Rose to take the time off.

Rose told Paul that she would take the train the next day.

And now here she was. Paul looked the picture of success in his crisp gray suit, but he embraced her and held on like a scared little boy. He was trembling ever so slightly, and his eyes had circles under them, like he hadn't slept well.

Paul took her bag and led her to the parking lot, where his new Packard gleamed in the sun. Sleek and long, with an olive green body and chrome trimmings, the top was down to reveal red leather seats and a polished wood dashboard.

"You're traveling in style, I see," Rose said, when they were on the road.

"Packard is one of my biggest customers," Paul said. "I think it's only fair that I use their products. It's good for business."

Paul had always been the clever one. He had his father's charm and fondness for risk-taking, although it was tempered by Rose's practical side. Paul would never take the kind of risks that would get him in trouble, the way Tim did. It was the right combination of personality traits to make him successful, and Rose was happy that his life had turned out so well.

Or, at least it had until now. This problem with Lucy was the first time in years that anything had gone seriously wrong for Paul, and she could tell he was unmoored, shaken by it.

"I don't know what to do," he said, bringing the subject up immediately. "Sometimes I think she hates me. I try to be sympathetic, but whatever I say makes her angry. I know it's been a difficult time for her, losing the baby like that, but I'm hurting too, you know. I've tried to keep busy, and I've thrown myself into some projects that are keeping me at the office pretty late. I've been traveling also. I have a big account in Pittsburgh, and I take the train out there every other week. You can't let things defeat you. I'd rather focus on the future. I mean, look at all this: we have a pretty good life out here."

Rose watched the landscape passing by and marveled at the beauty of it. The Quakers and the Germans who had first settled this land built simple stone farmhouses that had lasted for two hundred years, and it was beautiful to come over a hill and see the green fields and the herds of black and white milk cows and a white farmhouse silhouetted against the endless blue sky. As they got closer to Cheltenham the farms were replaced by tidy stone houses in various styles, and Rose saw the golf course with its perfectly manicured greens, with groups of men in their gaudy shirts and knickers playing the holes.

"Perhaps she just needs more time," Rose said. "It takes time to get over these things, Paul."

"Time is one thing we never get enough of, isn't that what you always told us?" Paul said. "I'd like to move on, try to have more children. I can't mourn that baby my whole life."

Paul turned onto a leafy street where the houses were larger and were surrounded by spacious lots. "Well, I'm glad you're here, Mother. Maybe you can help us fix this situation." He turned down a long gravel driveway that led up to a gabled stone house with a wraparound porch, big windows with blue shutters, and red azaleas blooming all around it. There was someone sitting on a rocking chair on the porch. It was Lucy, Rose realized, although there was something different about her.

"There she is," Paul said. There was a desperation in his voice that Rose hadn't heard before, and she realized that things must be worse than he was letting on. She should have known just from the fact that he asked her to visit; Lucy had never been fond of her, Rose knew, and there must have been something seriously wrong for Paul to invite her to stay.

Paul parked the car at the end of the driveway. He came around and held the door for Rose, and then he took her arm and helped her up the three steps to the porch.

Lucy did not acknowledge them. She was staring out at the lawn, smoking a cigarette, wearing what looked like a flimsy negligee. She still had some of the weight from her pregnancy, and her body spilled out of the dressing gown as if it could not be held back. Her hair was in a short bob, and it had been bleached blonde.

"Hello, darling," Paul said, walking over to her. He tried to kiss her on the cheek, but she turned her head away. "How are you this morning?"

There was a silence. Then, "What is she doing here?" Lucy said.

Rose realized that Paul hadn't told Lucy she was coming. This was not a good way to start things.

"I invited her to stay with us for a few days," Paul said. "I have to take the train to Pittsburgh this afternoon, and I thought she could stay with you. I thought you might like the company."

"Oh, you did?" Lucy sneered. "You thought I might like the company? You didn't ask me, you just assumed I would want to have her staying in my house. That's so typical of you, to decide what I might want."

There was an uncomfortable silence. "Maybe it's best that I leave," Rose said. "Come, Paul, you can take me back to the train station."

She started for the steps, but Paul grabbed her arm. "No," he said. "I want — I need you here, Mother. This is important to me."

The force with which he gripped her arm, and the note of desperation in his voice, made her stop. He looked like he was ready to fall apart.

"All right," Rose said. "If you need me, I'll stay."

Paul took her upstairs to her room, which was next to the room that had been little Claire's nursery. It was months since the baby died, but the room was still decorated in pink and white, with a white crib and paintings of cherubs on the wall, dolls and toys scattered about on chairs, and fresh flowers everywhere. It was obvious that Lucy was keeping this room as a shrine to Claire.

When Rose came downstairs Paul was in the kitchen, and he made a lunch of chicken sandwiches and coffee for her. Lucy stayed on the porch smoking, and they ate in silence. Rose could see that Paul was distressed by this situation, although he tried to keep the conversation focused on his successes at work. He rambled on about one project after another, going into great detail about his conversations with his clients and how he snagged one big account after another for the paper company, but it all rang hollow. Rose could see the worry in his eyes, and she felt sorry for him.

When he left to go to the train station he gave Rose an embrace and she felt the trembling in his body. He went out on the porch to say goodbye to Lucy, but she said nothing in reply. Rose heard the Packard drive off, and then there was silence.

She busied herself in the kitchen, looking about to find ingredients to make dinner later on, but all the while she wondered when Lucy would come in.

An hour went by, and then she heard a car drive up. She heard the car door open, and the crunch of shoes on the gravel, then a man's voice. She could not make out all the words, but there was a note of familiarity, of intimacy, that she did not like. Lucy's voice in reply was purring, teasing, gay — a very different tone than she'd used with Paul.

Rose made her way to the front of the house to get a look at this man. She came to the sitting room where the big windows looked out on the porch, and she saw a man in a golfing outfit of a lime green sweater, yellow knickers and red Argyll knee socks with white shoes, sitting close to Lucy in a rocking chair. He had short blonde hair and a golden tan, as if he'd spent many hours in the sun, and his white teeth glittered when he laughed, which he was doing now. He was sitting close to Lucy and had his hand on her knee.

Rose went out on the porch.

"Hello," she said. "May I ask who you are?"

The man turned with a look of surprise on his face, although he showed her his white teeth in a polite smile.

Lucy looked angry at being interrupted. "This is a friend of mine," she said. "His name is Harry Rawlins. He is the golf pro at our local club. Harry, this is my mother-in-law, Rose Morley."

"Pleased to meet you," Harry said. Rose noted that he hadn't offered his hand or stood up when she came onto the porch. He simply sat there staring at her as if he wished she would disappear. Lucy was looking at her sullenly, as if she also wanted Rose to vanish. There was an air of intimacy between them that Rose could almost smell.

"You must be tired from your train journey, Rose," Lucy said. "Why don't you go upstairs and take a nap?"

"I am not tired," Rose said, sitting down on a chair opposite them. "I think I will just sit here awhile."

There was a silence, when Rose felt them both looking for the words to get her to leave.

Finally, she said, "Young man, you've told me who you are, but what exactly are you doing here?"

Harry smiled, cleared his throat, and said, "Well, aren't we being presumptive? I don't remember hearing that you were Lucy's caretaker."

"She's not," Lucy said. "Even my own mother wouldn't ask a question like that. Actually, my mother wouldn't have anything to do with her."

"I am the mother of her husband," Rose said. "And I ask you again what you are doing here."

"You have no right to interrogate my friend like he's a common criminal," Lucy said.

"No, my dear, I have every right," Rose said. "Now, tell me, what are you doing here?" she said again, turning to Harry.

"I am visiting my friend," Harry said. "I am a good friend to Lucy." He drew himself up in the chair, like a peacock showing its tail. "I daresay a better friend than your son has been in her hour of need."

"No," Rose said, leaning close and staring directly at him. "You are not a friend. You are a mean, grasping man, a snake, and a deceiver. You want to steal something precious from my son, and you have come here while he is away, like a thief in the night. I have known men like you, and I have no doubt you will disappear as soon as you get what you want. You will not be here when Lucy cries out in the night for someone, when she grabs for a lifeline as she is sinking into the sea, as she tries to find something to hold onto to keep her mind from cracking. You will be long gone by then, Mister Rawlins, and Lucy will be lost and alone, amid the wreckage you have left behind. You have not come to help but to hurt her in ways that she cannot even imagine right now. Then too, I see a wedding ring on your finger. You are putting something in motion that will destroy many lives, and you sit there with a smug grin on your face like you're just passing the time of day."

Harry's eyes widened in surprise, and he took his hand away from Lucy's knee.

"You would do well to leave now," Rose said. "Because I am not a woman to be trifled with, lad. I will sooner see you destroyed than let you destroy my son's marriage. I will find that woman you're married to and tell her, and tell this whole town what you're doing, and you will have to say goodbye to the cozy little life you have here."

Harry looked at Lucy. Her mouth was set in a sullen line, but her eyes looked bewildered. Harry started to protest, but Rose put her hand up and stopped him.

"Think before you speak, lad," she said. "I am a crazy old Irishwoman, and I know many things you do not." She spoke a few sentences in her mother's singsong Irish brogue, a curse in the Ould Language, with enough menace in it that on some deep subconscious level he felt the raw fury she was sending toward him.

It worked. Harry gripped the arms of his chair and stiffened, his head leaning back like someone had just waved a loaded gun under his nose, and then he got up quickly. He turned to Lucy, and said, "That woman is crazy!" and bounded off the porch. He ran to his snappy yellow roadster, got in and started it, and reversed the car down the driveway in a flash, his wheels scattering gravel everywhere.

Rose watched him drive away, smiling.

She waited until the sound of screeching tires and the racing engine had faded completely. Then she turned to Lucy and said: "Now, my dear, we need to talk."

"I'm not talking to you," Lucy said, lighting another cigarette with a shaky hand. Rose noticed that her fingers were yellow from tobacco, and her negligee had stains on it, as if she'd spilled drinks on it. "Why don't you just go home?" Lucy said, exhaling cigarette smoke. "You're not needed here."

"Oh, but I am," Rose said. "Anytime my son's wife is entertaining men friends on the front porch of her house, I think I am definitely needed."

"He is the only person who understands me," Lucy whined. "Harry is a kind man, and he is someone I can talk to about my problem. I don't get any sympathy from Paul. All he's interested in is working more hours at my father's damned company. Sometimes I think he cares more about that company than me."

"I'm sorry about that," Rose said. "But maybe that's his way of dealing with his sadness."

Lucy's lip quivered, and her eyes brimmed with tears. "He can't be any sadder than me," she cried. "I'm the mother. I lost a baby, my darling little Claire. Can't you understand that? My world has been shattered, and all he can think about is selling more paper. I think I hate him now. There are times when I wish he were dead." She put her head in her hands and started weeping, her body racked with deep sobs.

Rose got up from the chair and went over and slapped her so hard Lucy lurched forward and almost toppled over, and her glass went clattering across the porch floor.

Rose was so angry she was shaking, and she stood over Lucy and shook her finger at her. "Now you listen to me, young lady. I don't want to hear any more of that kind of talk. You lost a baby, and that's a tragedy, but you're not to let it overmaster you. Do you hear me? Why, if I let every tragedy that happened in my life put me in a state like you're in, I'd have curled up and died years ago.

"Life knocks you off your feet now and then," Rose continued. "And that's just the way it is. I don't know why God lets these things happen, but He does, and there's no use crying about it. When they happen, you have two choices: Either you crawl away like a dog that's been whipped, or you get up and put your life back together as best you can. There's no man out there who will make the pain go away, Lucy, so get that out of your head. You must heal yourself, and start anew. Paul is feeling just as devastated as you are, but he's trying to deal with it by drowning himself in work. He needs you now, and if you go to him and help him get better, it will help your heart to heal as well."

"But I'm in pain," Lucy said. She had stopped weeping, but her face was glistening with tears and her eyes looked wounded and afraid.

Rose took her by the shoulders. "We are all in pain, child. Life is pain. Maybe you did not know that, but you're learning it now. You can only deal with it by looking at it square in the face, not by trying to lose yourself in fantasies. Pray, pray to God, but do more than that: get up and tell your husband you love him. Hold on to him for dear life, for he's the most precious thing a woman can have — a man who loves her with his whole being. He will repay you a thousand times over for it, I promise you, Lucy."

Lucy looked up at Rose and a light seemed to dawn in her eyes. She looked at Rose with a new respect, even affection. She stood up and said, "Would you hold me, Rose?"

Rose embraced her and held her for a long time, stroking her hair and telling her everything was going to be all right. Lucy cried one last time for her lost little girl, but then she sighed and straightened up.

"I don't want to be in that darkness anymore," she said. "I felt like I was being sucked down a whirlpool, and I couldn't get out. I'm going to go in and get changed now." She squared her shoulders and started to head toward the front door. She turned, though, and came back and took Rose by the hand. "Thank you," she said. Then she turned and went in the house.

Rose sat back down on the rocking chair and looked out at the perfectly manicured lawn. Her son had come a long way, and she was happy for him. Who would have thought that Rose Sullivan from Skibbereen would have a son who lived in this grand fashion? Ah, but even the grandest people still have problems, don't they? They still go to bed at night with their fears and their sadnesses, and they lie there at 3 AM and wonder how they can get up the next morning and face the day.

She looked at the wedding ring on her finger, and thought about Martin. You've given me much heartache, God, she thought, and I've railed against you time and again. But you gave me a precious gift of a man in Martin Lancaster, and I thank you for it. And this girl will be all right, for she's got the same stuff in her, the same goodness, as my Paul. But please, give them a child soon — a new baby to wipe away the tears from saying goodbye to the last one.

CHAPTER SIXTEEN

October 1929

James stopped the car at the top of a little hill a mile from the farmhouse and got out. The sun had gone down a half hour before but the sky in the West was still lit with a deep orange afterglow and he could see the cars surrounding the farmhouse, and across the open fields he could hear the pop of gunfire coming from the house.

By now O'Toole and his men could be dead, or at least badly wounded. James had a feeling of lightness, a mad exuberance that made him want to dance on the top of the hill.

He had escaped the disaster he thought was waiting for him all these years. He had gone to work for O'Toole and built up a successful bootlegging operation out here in the remote part of Delaware, and he'd made some money from it, but he had always dreaded the day when it would all come crashing down.

The bigger they got, the more customers they had, the more he feared attracting the attention of the authorities. O'Toole was paying a lot of people off, but James figured somewhere, someone would rat on them, and then the police would show up just like this, with guns drawn and ready for violence.

So, he beat them to it. He arranged to meet a Bureau Of Investigation agent in downtown Wilmington, at a little lunch counter near the busy train station, and he told the man everything. He handed over an account book with names, dates and numbers, and the agent's eyes widened as he looked at the names of some of the prominent members of Society from up and down the East Coast who'd bought illegal liquor from O'Toole's operation.

"This is going to be a big catch," the agent said, rubbing his hands together gleefully. "I'll get a promotion for this one."

"Remember," James said. "The deal is that my son Tim and I are not part of it. You only go after O'Toole and his men. I'll get word to you when Tim is out of town, and that's when you'll raid the place."

"You have my word," the agent said. "Besides, O'Toole is the big fish. He's got his hands in every bootlegging operation from Philadelphia down to Baltimore. He's a nasty piece of work, that one. I have to ask: Aren't you worried he'll come after you? If he doesn't get killed when we raid the place he'll try to get his revenge on you. He's an Irishman like you, and you people are masters at carrying grudges."

"I'll be long gone," James said. "I've put some money away, and I'm ready to move on. I'll be leaving the area. Doing a little traveling. I've taken it in mind to pay a visit to my home town in Ireland."

"Let the local yokels see how well you've done, eh?" the agent said. "Show them what a success you've become in America?"

"Something like that," James said. "I was never interested in going back before. I didn't care to see any of those people again. But enough time has gone by, and I think I'd like to see the old place once more before I die. And yes, I'll be playing the part of the rich American cousin."

"Rich". That was a word he'd never applied to himself before. He had made $25,000 investing in the stock market, and for the first time in his life James felt flush with cash. He had enough to move to an apartment in the Rittenhouse Hotel, where he stayed when he visited Philadelphia. He had enough to buy a Packard roadster, and he had enough to distribute to the important people in his life.

Like Edith. She was living in a small apartment in Philadelphia, working as a saleswoman in a candy store. Despite James's constant entreaties she had never let him come back and live as her husband. Over the years she had gradually warmed up to him enough that she would meet him for lunch occasionally or take a walk down by the river on a sunny afternoon. She kept an invisible wall between them, though, and although their conversations were polite and she even seemed concerned about his welfare, she never let him kiss her.

He liked to give her gifts with his newfound money. He bought her little presents and gave them to her on their outings. She would not let him spend too much, and never anything as nice as jewelry or even gifts of cash, but she would accept something small like a scarf, or a bouquet of flowers, or perhaps a box of chocolates. She gave him the news of his children, for Mercy and John would still not have anything to do with him. Mercy was married with two children now, and James knew she lived outside the city in a western suburb. He delighted in buying gifts for her children, toy soldiers and dolls and such, and leaving them on her doorstep after dark. Edith would tell him about these strange gifts that Mercy was receiving, and James always had a feeling that she had figured out what he was doing and was somehow cooperating in the deception.

Then there was the other deception, with Rose. He had found out from Tim where Rose lived, which was a modest row house in the city, where she lived with her second husband, Martin Lancaster. Tim had said that Lancaster had been disowned by his family, and he was working as a criminal lawyer, defending petty lawbreakers who had very little money to pay him. James knew some of these people — he'd found that once he was involved with Aloysius O'Toole he had access to the city's underworld of thieves, con artists, bootleggers, and other shady characters — and when he heard that Martin Lancaster was defending one of them he made sure to give the man an envelope of cash to pay Lancaster with. He expected that they'd take a little cut for themselves, but he trusted them — mostly because they were afraid of what O'Toole would do to them if they crossed James — and they always delivered the money. He felt good knowing that he was helping Martin to support Rose.

Then there was Tim. James didn't know what his son's life would be like now if it weren't for him. Tim was sick a lot with chest ailments, and he had a cough that never seemed to go away. He was a low level member of O'Toole's operation, a functionary who delivered the bootleg liquor to the houses of the rich for their fancy parties. O'Toole trusted him with money, and although Tim tended to take a nip of the liquor whenever he could, it didn't seem to bother O'Toole. Tim had the sallow look of someone who was sick, and he had a scowl on his face and bleary eyes most of the time. He lived in James's apartment on Rittenhouse Square, and although the staff didn't appreciate having someone with Tim's down at heels look in their building, James's habit of tipping them liberally helped to make the situation more palatable to them.

For the first time in his life James felt like a person of substance. He was no longer the miserable orphan boy from Tullamore, nor the driver of the rich in America, nor the bit player in Siegmund Lubin's motion pictures — he was a man of means now, and he took pleasure in the way people paid attention to him when he took a wad of cash from his pocket. He liked what he could do with the money, liked that he could make a difference in people's lives with it.

He got back in the car and started it again, admiring the

purr of the engine, the leather seats, the gauges and buttons on the dashboard, and all the trappings of a gentleman's car. He started down the bumpy dirt road with the sound of gunfire fading in the distance.

He had told O'Toole he was driving back to Philadelphia for a few days, that he needed a rest after making the latest batch of liquor. The old scoundrel had frowned and told him there were customers waiting for the next batch, but he knew that James was irreplaceable and he had no choice but to let him go for a few days.

Now he was probably dead. O'Toole might have wanted to buy time by surrendering to the federal agents, but some of his men were hotheads who would just as soon shoot it out with them. All that gunfire meant that the hotheads had prevailed, and the angel of Death had visited the farmhouse.

James had no remorse about that. O'Toole was a bad man, and he was only getting his just punishment. James fully expected to get his own punishment when he died, for the crime he had committed so many years ago in Ireland.

But maybe he could make amends, at least in some partial way, for what he'd done. He had gotten the idea in recent months that he could go back, revisit his homeland, and maybe do some good with the money he'd made. Maybe he could find some poor boy like himself fifty years ago and provide for his education. Maybe he could buy a farm for some miserable family that had never owned an inch of ground in their lives. Maybe he could give money to build a school, or a church, or something like that. Ireland had just received its independence two years ago, but he knew from talking to immigrants it was a scarred, threadbare, broken land and the people in it walked like ghosts among the ruined towns and empty farms. He would go back, a different person than the frightened boy who'd run away so many years ago, a triumphant man who returned bearing gifts.

He would call his broker in the morning and sell all his stock. He would walk away with a check for thousands of dollars, and he would use some of it to buy a few final gifts for the important people in his life. He planned to tell Tim everything he'd done, and recommend that he move out of town for a few years. He would give him plenty of money to live on, and he hoped that Tim would move to someplace warm and dry, like Arizona, where the climate might be better for his damaged lungs. Tim might be angry that his source of liquor had dried up, but James felt sure he would understand this was the best plan for the long run.

It was all working out so nicely, James thought, as he saw the lights of Philadelphia come into view. For once in his life, he had done something that was going to work out. He remembered the darkness of the fields at night during his youth, the pitch black with only the stars to light his way when he was walking to the Army barracks before sunrise to feed the horses their breakfast. It was a time before electricity, and now look, he was living in this world of brilliant light at night time, this world of automobiles and telephones and flying machines and mechanical marvels he had not dreamed of as a boy.

As he drove down Walnut street it was almost midnight, and there were still a few people on the street, some men and women in fancy clothes laughing and stumbling a bit from the alcohol they'd drunk at one of the speakeasies the police were pretending not to notice. Thanks to you for your thirst, James thought, for it's that has put money in my pocket.

He parked the Packard in a garage across the street from the Rittenhouse Hotel and went across and greeted the doorman, a big Irishman in a blue greatcoat with gold braid named Clancy who liked to keep James informed of the news in the great world of finance.

"Good evening, Mr. Francis," Clancy said, tipping his hat. "Coming home late tonight, I see?"

"Oh, just some business that kept me up," James said, stopping for a chat. "What's the news tonight, Clancy?"

Clancy's brow furrowed. "You haven't seen a newspaper?"

"No I've been so hard at work I feel like I've been in a cocoon for the last week."

"Why, the stock market's crashed, man," Clancy said. "It's a disaster, to be sure. There's many a man out there who's been ruined."

"Crashed?" James said. "What do you mean, crashed?"

"The prices have taken a terrible fall," Clancy said. "They're so far down the stocks are selling for pennies, and that's the blue chip ones. Most of it is worthless now. Why, I bought a few shares meself last June, paid good money for it, and my broker tells me I might as well use the certificates to wrap fish in, for all they're worth now."

"It'll come back," James said. "It always does, doesn't it?"

"Not according to the fellows on Wall Street," Clancy said. "The newspapers say it's a worldwide crisis, and all the speculation of the last few years has caused it. I think we're in for a good long run of bad luck, Mr. Francis."

"Nonsense, Clancy," James said. "Don't you let those newspapers upset your digestion. You can't believe everything you read in them." He tipped his hat and went in the door, but behind his jaunty facade he had a feeling that his life would be changing once again.

CHAPTER SEVENTEEN

December 24, 1931

"Tim is sick, Rose. He's in the Jefferson Hospital, and they don't think he's going to make it."

Martin had come to her with that news as she was preparing to visit Paul's family for Christmas. She was due to take the 2:00 train to Cheltenham and spend Christmas Eve with Paul and Lucy and their two year old daughter Rose. The child was the delight of Rose's life, and she had looked forward to this visit all week. Martin was tied up in court and was going to come after dinner on a later train.

When Rose saw Martin come in the door of their home she knew something was wrong. He never came home early from the courts, not even on Christmas Eve. There was always someone in trouble he had to attend to. He was more than a lawyer for his clients: he loaned them money, found them places to live, found jobs for them when they wanted to go straight, tried to keep them off the booze, wrote their letters for them, bought them clothes for their court appearances, fed them when they needed a square meal. He never made much money from them, but he seemed happier than he had ever been, much happier than when he had lived in the big house in Chestnut Hill with his parents and the servants where Rose first met him so many years ago.

For years Martin had kept tabs on Tim through his network of contacts among the police and the underworld in the city, and he let Rose know what was happening with her son. She knew that Tim had been living with his father in a rundown rooming house, which was all they could afford. Martin had told her that Peter was calling himself James Francis these days, and that he had a job as a janitor at the Reading Terminal train station two days a week, where he made a few dollars. He was a lucky man to have any job at all, because there were millions of people out of work and jobs were hard to come by. Tim, well, no one knew just exactly how he made the pitiful amount of money he lived on. He was sick or drunk most of the time. Rose took him food and money when she visited him once a week, always on a day when she knew his father would not be there.

Now the day she had feared had arrived. She had been expecting to hear that he had come to a bad end, perhaps beaten to death by someone he owed money to, or frozen to death where he had passed out in a gutter in some alley where no one would find him in time.

"He's got pneumonia," Martin said. "A friend of mine on the police force told me they took him in an ambulance last night. He's having trouble breathing, and they can't do much for him."

"Take me to him," Rose said.

Martin did not have a car, so they rode the subway down to the hospital, and got out and walked up to the street level, making their way through the merry holiday crowds and the carolers and the bright lights. The country was going through bad times, and there were many people out of work, but somehow it seemed that Christmas still put a smile on people's faces. They went up the stone steps to the hospital, and inside the tiled marble lobby there were receptionists behind a counter. The place looked like a hotel, all gleaming surfaces and polished wood.

Tim was in a room at the end of a long hallway on the third floor, and when Rose and Martin entered she let out a sob. Tim was lying in a bed, his breath coming in long wheezing rasps, a nurse in a pointed white cap and starched white uniform sitting next to him, and when she turned to Rose and Martin it was clear she did not think there was much time left.

"May I sit with him?" Rose said. "I am his mother."

"Yes, of course," the nurse said. "I have been putting wet compresses on his forehead." She pointed to a basin with wet washcloths in ice water. "He has a terribly high fever."

"I can do that," Rose said. "Thank you. You may go."

The nurse seemed surprised by Rose's peremptory manner, but she got up and left the room. Rose sat down and stroked Tim's forehead. It felt as hot as the coals from a fireplace. His eyes were closed, and his lips were dry. He seemed agitated, and every once in a while his legs thrashed about under the covers. He was terribly thin, and his skin looked like old parchment.

"I'll leave you alone," Martin said. "I'll go downstairs and walk around. I'll be back to check on you in an hour."

When he left, Rose talked to Tim, her voice low and reassuring.

"Ah, my darling boy," she said. "Sorry I am for everything that's happened, dearest one. You've had the devil's own time of it, ever since you were born. I used to look at you and wonder how you stood it, and maybe it's not so bad that you'll have some rest now. I don't know why it's all turned out like this, and if I could make it right I would. I wish we could all start over, oh how I wish for that! It's not the way of things, though. We get one chance, and we make of it what we will. I hope you had some happiness, though. I hope you had the moments when you knew you were happy, those magical moments when it all comes together and we get a glimpse of what Heaven must be like. For there is a glimmer sometimes, my boy, and that's all that keeps us going. A glimmer of another world, another place, a hint that there's something more than this vale of tears."

Tim's eyes flickered but did not open, but just then a smile found its way to his lips, and Rose felt he'd heard her. It was a smile of benediction, a smile that told her maybe he had a place in his soul that was not dead, a place of hope, a refuge from the anger and bitterness.

She did not know how long she sat there. Martin came back from time to time, but mostly he let her sit with her son, whispering and singing to him, sometimes in the ould tongue, the songs and rhymes her mother taught her so many years ago.

Sometime in the evening, she heard a voice at her back. "Hello, Rose."

It was Peter. He was an old man, his black hair gone stark white, his face creased at the eyes and the corners of the mouth, his back no longer straight but stooped now like a man carrying a great load on his shoulders. He was rubbing his hands together nervously, and Rose felt a great pity come over her at the sight of him standing there as if he wanted to apologize for his very presence.

Can this be the boy who kissed me so long ago in Skibbereen? How he has changed!

"How is my son?" Peter said.

"See for yourself," Rose said, pointing to a wooden chair in the corner of the room. "Bring that chair over here."

Peter slid the chair over and sat down. His knees were touching Rose's. He did not seem to notice, though, for he was looking only at Tim. His eyes were pained, and he sighed deeply.

"It was my fear that this would happen," he said. "He was always so sick. And the drink only made it worse. He didn't eat enough to keep body and soul together. I could never get him to take more than a few mouthfuls of food, no matter how hard I tried."

He seemed to need to explain things to Rose. "The boy never came home last night. It happened before, so I didn't worry. I just thought he'd made a few dollars somehow and spent it drinking in one of the places he frequents. I don't ask too many questions. When I came downstairs this morning the landlady told me he'd come in late and collapsed inside the front door of the building. I heard the ambulance last night, but I didn't think it was for Tim."

"Things never went easy for him," Rose said. "Everything seemed to turn out wrong."

"It's me who's to blame for this," Peter said. "I did wrong by the boy, and all of you. I ruined things for you."

He wrung his hands in his lap, the picture of helplessness, and Rose felt sorry for him.

"It's a long time ago, all that," Rose said. "We were a lot younger then. You call yourself by a different name now, I'm told, so you've moved on. But there's no getting away from the past, is there? We make our mistakes; we pick up the pieces and carry them with us, but we move on."

"Ah, but it wouldn't be so bad if there weren't other souls involved," Peter said, pointing at Tim's feverish body. "We never realize how many people are touched by our lives, do we? Why, you can't turn around in this life without bumping into someone and causing them to stumble. We're all connected, like horses in harness, only we don't know it."

Rose took the washcloth from Tim's forehead, rinsed it out in the basin of cold water, and put it back, putting her hand on Tim's cheek to calm him. He was struggling, and you could hear the fluid in his lungs as he gasped for each breath.

"He's burning up," she said. "Lord, I wish there was something I could do for him."

"There's not a blessed thing we can do," Peter said. Then, his face brightened. "Do you think he'd hear me if I sang a song?" It was clear he was doing it for himself as much as for Tim. Rose realized that performing was his first response to every crisis. He was more comfortable putting on a show than being himself.

"I don't see why not," Rose said. "Hearing you sing might do him good."

"Do you remember this one?" Peter said. "I sang it to you long ago, Rose Sullivan." He sang:

> 'O Father dear, I often hear you speak of Erin's Isle,
> Her lofty scenes, her valleys green, her mountains rude and wild.
> They say it is a lovely land wherein a saint might dwell;
> Oh why did you abandon it? The reason, to me tell.'

His voice was still clear and pure, although it came from a face that was creased and worn and the blue eyes were dimmed with sadness.

> 'O son, I loved my native land with energy and pride
> 'Til a blight came o'er my crops, my sheep and cattle died
> My rent and taxes were too high, I could not them redeem
> And that's the cruel reason that I left old Skibbereen.
> 'O well do I remember the bleak December day
> The landlord and the sheriff came to drive us all away;
> They set my roof on fire with cursed English spleen,
> And that's another reason that I left old Skibbereen.
> 'Your mother too, God rest her soul, fell on the snowy ground,
> She fainted in her anguish, seeing the desolation round;
> She never rose, but passed away from life to mortal dream
> And found a quiet grave, my boy, in dear old Skibbereen.
> 'And you were only two years old and feeble was your frame
> I could not leave you with my friends, you bore your father's
>   name;

*I wrapped you in my cothamore at the dead of night unseen,
I heaved a sigh and bade good-bye to dear old Skibbereen.'"*

When he ended on a high note he put his head down and was silent. Rose could not speak for a few moments, and it seemed that the note echoed in the stillness of the room.

"I never went back," Rose said, finally.

"Nor did I," Peter said. "I often wonder what the old place looks like."

"It's changed," Rose said. "There's no one left in my family. The farm was sold. Everything we knew is gone."

"It's the way of things, isn't it?" Peter said. "Nothing stays the same, no matter how much we want it to."

He stood up, and put a hand on Rose's shoulder. "I will be leaving now, Rose. I cannot stay and watch my son leave this mortal world. It is not a thing I am able to do."

For a moment, Rose thought he would bend over and kiss her, but instead he leaned over the bed and kissed Tim on the cheek. He whispered something in Tim's ear, then turned and walked out of the room.

It was so like him, Rose thought, to leave just when she needed someone to lean on. Ah, what should I have expected, she told herself. He was never more than a hole in my life, more of an absence than a presence even in the best of times. No use crying about him.

"Are you all right, Rose?" Martin said. He was standing in the doorway, and somehow Rose knew that he had been there for a long while, and had heard everything that transpired between Peter and her.

She looked at his kind face, the love that had never wavered, even though he had sacrificed everything for it, and she said, "I am fine now that you are here, Martin Lancaster."

CHAPTER EIGHTEEN

July 1, 1933

"Bless me, Father, for I have sinned," James said. "It has been more than 50 years since I have been to Confession."

There was silence in the dark confessional, and James heard the priest behind the screen shift his body and clear his throat. "Did you say 50 years?"

"Yes, Father. I have been a long time away from the sacraments."

"You certainly have. Did you not pass a church in all those years?"

"Many times, Father. I even went in once or twice, but I lost my nerve before I could get to the confessional."

"What brings you here today?"

"Well, to be honest, Father, I am very sick and I don't have long to live. I have a stomach ailment, you see, and the doctor says it's the cancer. There's nothing much they can do for me, and I suppose I'd like to get some things off my chest."

"Coming back to God at the end of your days, are you? Well, better late than never, my son. Go ahead now and make a good Confession."

"Thank you, Father." James had lain awake for several nights cataloguing his sins of the past half century, and it was a long list indeed. The venial sins were too numerous to mention, so he figured he'd stick to the mortal ones, and of those he had a good-sized list. He had committed adultery, had made and sold bootleg liquor, had committed sexual sins, had missed Sunday Mass for most of his adult life, had lied thousands upon thousands of times, had deceived and betrayed and abandoned the people closest to him, and also, he could not forget, had murdered someone.

That was the clincher. It would be embarrassing to spell out his other sins, to go into detail about all his many failings, but the murder was something he shuddered to think about saying out loud. He practiced it, trying to sandwich it in between his other sins so that it would not stand out so much.

When it came time, however, when he had drawn to the end of his list of transgressions, and the priest said, "Is there anything else?" he froze.

He could feel cold drops of sweat on his forehead, and he moved his mouth, trying to make the words come out.

Nothing happened.

"Did you not hear me, man?" the priest said. " I asked if there was anything else."

"No," James blurted out. "That's all, Father."

He barely heard the priest's words of benediction, nor his encouragement to receive the Grace of the confessional more frequently, nor the instructions to say three Hail Marys for his penance, and he stumbled through the Act of Contrition, then blessed himself, said, "Thank you, Father," and lurched out of the confessional, a stricken man.

What will I do? I have compounded my sins by not confessing the biggest sin of all. I have lied to a priest in the house of the Lord. I will die without absolution, and my soul will spend eternity tormented by the fires of Hell, all because of my cowardice.

He knelt in a pew near the side altar and in the half light of the church he looked up at a statue of St. Thomas the Apostle, a bearded man in flowing robes who seemed to have kind eyes.

James couldn't recall the story about him. Was he the one who denied Jesus three times? No, that didn't seem right. He remembered a story about Doubting Thomas, who would not believe that Jesus was resurrected until he put his fingers into the Lord's wounds.

Well, it doesn't matter if you denied Jesus or doubted Him, James prayed. It just shows you were a human being like me, with the same failings. Maybe you can understand how a person can make such a mess of his life. Faith, I don't know I got to this point from where I started, poor, barefoot Sean McCarthy in Tullamore. I've had my share of ups and downs, some songs and laughter along the way, but sure and I've hurt a lot of people too. Maybe you can put a good word in for me with your boss, for I could badly use it. I'm in a sorry state: I need forgiveness for my sin, but I can't ask the priest for it. I'll be damned forever if I die a sinner. What do I do?

James listened for an answer, but there was only the hum of automobiles and buses out in the street. The world was hurrying by out there, not caring about him and his problems, or that he would soon be taking his leave of it.

He had a pain in his stomach that would not go away, and it was killing him. There were tumors growing in him, the doctor said, but they could not operate because he was too old and the surgeons couldn't guarantee they'd get all the tumors anyway. "There's nothing we can do," Doctor Zimmer said. "You should get your affairs in order."

How much time did he have? Not long, he feared. The pain had grown for months before he finally went to the doctor. There was swelling in his belly that was getting bigger, and when Doctor Zimmer saw it he frowned. James spent a night in the hospital, tests were done, but the news was not good.

"Get your affairs in order." What affairs? His life was a small thing now, confined to the room he had shared with Tim, and he spent most of his days there since he had become too weak to work anymore.

He lost almost all his money in the stock market crash, and he was running out of the little he had left. He would not ask Edith for help, nor Rose. Neither of them had much to spare anyway. Then the thought came to him: Paul. Paul never wanted to have any contact with him, but he had kept up on Paul's life through Tim. He knew that Paul was married with two children, that he lived in a town called Cheltenham, and that he had become very successful. Maybe Paul would help.

But how? With money? Paul would probably not want to give him a cent. He'll be bitter because of what I did, James thought, looking at the statue again. Can you blame him? I did him wrong, and he can't forget that. I took his childhood away from him. Maybe he'll throw me out on my ear if I go to him.

Then it came to him: I'll ask for no money from him. No, I'll confess my sin to him. It will give me peace, and maybe it will help him to understand the scoundrel he has for a father.

It was a plan, and James felt better that at least he had some kind of a plan. He looked up at the statue again, and said: "Thank you. I don't know if it was you that put that idea in my head, but if it was, I thank you, my good man." He got out of the pew, genuflected, and went out into the busy, uncaring city.

He did not delay, but went straight to the corner and found a phone booth, where he looked up the name "Paul Morley" in the phone book hanging from a cord. There were two Paul Morleys listed, but only one in Cheltenham, at 75 Lilac Lane. That had to be him.

James took the subway to the Reading Terminal and bought a ticket on a 5:00 train to Cheltenham. It was already 4:00, so he passed the time on a bench, watching the commuters hurrying to and from their trains, all eager to get somewhere fast. There was a time when his life was measured by the slow, deliberate plodding of horses, but now it was racing like an automobile headed straight down a steep hill. There were men standing near the train platforms holding signs saying, "Out of work. Please help," and once in awhile someone would drop a coin in their palm. There were so many people out of work, people dazed and confused like survivors of a shipwreck, washed up on a beach in a strange country. James didn't know this world anymore, it was so different than the one he'd grown up in.

There was a time when he was enraptured by the promise of the future, excited by what was coming just around the corner. Now the future had come, but he didn't like it at all. There seemed to be no place for him here.

He got on the train at 5:00 and watched the city tumble into suburbs as the train went on its way. He would be there in an hour; Cheltenham was not far, he knew. He was experiencing waves of pain in his stomach, a feeling like a hot poker being thrust into every corner of his insides. He had to clench his teeth sometimes, to keep from crying out. He tried to keep his mind busy to distract himself. How old would Paul's children be? He seemed to remember Tim saying there were two of them, a girl named Rose and a boy named Billy. It was wonderful that Paul had named a daughter Rose, after his mother. A good idea to keep that name alive, James thought. I wonder if she looks like her grandmother. He found himself looking forward to getting to meet his grandchildren for the first time.

When the train pulled into the Cheltenham station James got off and managed to find a cab driver, an enterprising teenager who had put a sign on an ancient Model T and set himself up to make a few dollars.

"Where to, Mister?" he said, helping James into the car.

"75 Lilac Lane," James said. "Do you know where that is?"

"Sure do," the boy said. "That's the better side of town.

Folks there live pretty well."

He was right, for when they got to that neighborhood James could see the houses were substantial and their yards spacious and well-tended, giving off an air of prosperity and good fortune. He was proud that Paul lived so well. He's living the life I wanted, James thought. Good for him.

As the car turned onto the long driveway and the house came into view, James saw a woman sitting on a porch swing reading a book to two small children. She was dressed in a white summer dress, and the blonde-haired children were dressed in white linen, with a dress for the little girl and short pants, knee socks and white shirt for the little boy. They got up from the swing and stared as the cab driver stopped at the end of the driveway.

"Momma, who's that?" James heard the little girl say, as he was paying the cab driver.

"I don't know, honey," the mother said.

The cab drove off and James made his way up the porch steps slowly, gasping a bit because of the pain in his insides. When he got to the top he leaned against the railing, holding on tightly and trying to stand straight and tall.

"Can I help you?" the woman said. The two children were standing at her side, holding on to her and looking at James as if they were afraid of him.

"I'm sorry to bother you," James said. "Is your husband home?"

"He will be home shortly," the woman said. "What do you want with him?"

"I just need to speak with him for a few minutes," James said. "I need to tell him. . . something." There was an awkward silence. "I'm his father."

The woman put her hand to her mouth. "You're. . . you're Rose's husband?"

"He's not grandma's husband, Momma," the little girl said. "She's married to Mr. Martin, not this man."

"Well, actually, grandma was married before," the woman said. "This is your father's father."

The little girl looked at James like he was some strange creature that had crawled onto her porch. She was repulsed, but more than a little curious.

Just then James doubled over, from a pain that stabbed him in the stomach, and he gasped for breath.

"Are you all right?" the woman said, coming over to him. "Please, sit down." She guided him over to the porch swing and helped him to sit. "Can I get anything for you? Do you want me to call a doctor?"

"No," James said, as the pain passed. "There's nothing a doctor can do. I'll be all right. Thank you for your kindness."

"What's your name?" the little girl said. She had left her mother's side and was standing right in front of him, staring at him as if she were deciding what to make of him.

"My name is James Francis," he said.

"Well, you can't be my Daddy's father, because his name is Paul Morley." She put her hands on her hips and stared at him triumphantly, as if she had him stumped.

"I used to call myself Peter Morley," he said. "And before that I was Sean McCarthy."

"That's silly," the girl said. "People should have one name. I'm Rose Morley. This is my brother Billy. My mother's name is Lucy Morley. We all have one first name and one last name. Why do you have so many names?"

James chuckled. "I don't know. It just happened, somehow. I agree with you, though, that it's a better policy to have just one name. It's too confusing to carry all these names around with you. I should have stuck with one."

"Why don't we get you some lemonade?" Rose said. "It's

hot outside, and my mother makes the very best lemonade."

"Yes," Lucy said. "Rose is right. Would you like some lemonade?"

Food and drink didn't interest him, but James did not want to disappoint them. "Of course," he said. "It sounds like a wonderful idea."

"I'll be right back," Lucy said. She went inside, leaving Rose and little Billy staring at James on the porch. Billy was sucking his thumb and holding Rose's hand, and she was examining James skeptically, like she still wasn't sure what to make of him.

"You look old," she said. "Your hair is white."

"Yes it is white," James said, running a hand through his hair. "And I am old. Sometimes I'm surprised at how old I am."

"I'm six years old," Rose said. "And Billy is three."

"Those are fine ages," James said. "Why, I'd give anything to be either of those ages again. You have your whole lives in front of you. Just think of the things you'll have seen by the time you get to be my age!"

Rose wrinkled her nose. "Your age? I'm not ever going to be your age. I don't want to be old and wrinkled like you. I'm going to stay six years old forever."

"Why, that's a capital idea," James said. "And I think you should stick with it. No sense in getting old if you can avoid it."

"Why aren't you still married to my grandma?"

James sighed. "Oh, it's a long story and hard to explain. I made some mistakes. I, ah, met someone else who captured my heart. It's not something you can understand unless you're a grownup."

Rose frowned and shook her head. It was obvious she thought the grownup world was full of absurdities, and this was one more proof of it.

"Come on, Billy, let's go inside and play," she said, tugging her brother by the arm. They started toward the door, but then there was the sound of a car coming down the driveway.

"Oh, look, Daddy's here," she said. Billy took his thumb out of his mouth and clapped his hands.

James watched as the gleaming blue Packard came purring down the drive and stopped noiselessly in front of the porch. The door opened and Paul got out. He was going gray around the temples, and he had the aura of casual success and wealth about him in his crisp seersucker suit and white straw hat. He bounded up the steps and took the two children in his arms, kissing and hugging them, before he saw James on the porch swing.

His face clouded and he put the children down quickly. "What are you doing here?" he demanded.

"Daddy, that man was married to grandma!" Rose said. "He came to see you."

Just then Lucy came out the door carrying a tray with a pitcher of lemonade and some glasses. She saw the look on Paul's face and she froze.

"Hello, Paul," James said. "You're looking well, my boy."

Paul's eyes narrowed, and he clenched his fists at his sides. "I'm asking you again: What are you doing here?"

A wave of pain hit James in the stomach once more, and he had to hold on to the arms of the swing to keep from doubling over. "I, ah, came to speak with you," he said. "I have something I need to talk to you about."

Paul's face was stony. He was a picture of cold fury, his mouth a tight line, the muscles in his jaw working furiously.

"Please," James said, trying hard not to cry out in pain. "It's important. I may not have much time."

"Paul, I think you should speak to your father," Lucy said. She set the tray down on a small table next to the porch swing and said, "Rose, bring Billy over here and we'll go inside. Your father needs some privacy."

Rose seemed mystified once again by the behavior of adults, but she took Billy's hand and followed her mother inside.

Paul came over to the swing and sat on a rocking chair across from James. He leaned forward and spoke low enough so that only James could hear: "I don't know what this is about, but you have a lot of gall showing up at my house, old man. I've half a mind to throw you off this porch, but I'll relent for Lucy's sake and give you ten minutes. After that, you're leaving. Do you understand?"

"Yes, of course," James said. "I understand."

"Now, what did you want to tell me?"

"I, ah," James began.

"Yes?" Paul said.

"I don't have long to live," James blurted out. "I have something wrong with my insides."

"I'm sorry," Paul said, curling his lip, "but if you expect me to have sympathy for you, there is none. That disappeared a long time ago. Now, if that's what you came to say. . ." he stood up.

"No, no," James said. "Please sit down. That wasn't it at all."

Paul sat down reluctantly. "All right, what is it?"

"I've made a lot of mistakes."

Paul snorted. "That's an understatement! You've made more mistakes than most, that's for sure. But again, if that's all you came to tell me, you might as well leave now. You're not telling me anything I didn't already know."

James sighed. "I went to Confession, but I couldn't bring myself to tell one of my sins."

Paul sat back in the rocking chair and folded his arms, waiting for more.

"I, I just couldn't tell the priest," James said. "But I don't want to die without telling someone. I thought I could tell you. . ."

Paul sneered. "Now I've heard everything! I'm your confessor? I'm not a priest, old man. And I'm not interested in helping you to die with a clear conscience. If it's forgiveness you're looking for, you won't get it from me."

"No," James said. "I know you won't forgive me for that. Although I wish I could explain it to you. I loved your mother, and still do. It was a hard life for us in those years, though. I didn't do my duty by you, and I'm sorry for that. Then, too, I fell in love with someone else. I don't expect you to understand that, Paul, but it's true. I couldn't help what happened—"

Paul's face reddened and he brought his fist down on the arm of the chair. "I've heard enough. You sit there and try to act like it's not your fault! You ruined our lives, dragged us through the mud. Do you have any idea of what it was like, how we struggled? We went to bed hungry many nights, and Mother never knew how she was going to pay the next month's rent. Tim got in fights every day at school because of the gossip the other children heard about us at home. He was called a bastard more times than I can count. We always hoped you would come back, but you never did. You didn't even show up at Tim's funeral, for god's sake." His face was red with rage but his eyes were misty and he fought to control himself.

"I couldn't bring myself to go to Tim's funeral," James said. "It was too painful. I lived with him the last five years, and every day I berated myself for what I did to him. I couldn't go and look at him in the casket."

Paul stood up again. "I'm finished with you. You've had your ten minutes, now leave. And don't ever come back."

"Please," James said. "I only need a few minutes more. It's something I need to tell you. Please."

Paul sat down slowly, looking at his watch. "I'm rapidly

running out of patience with you," he said.

"A long time ago. . ." James began. "Ah, I don't know how to say it, so I'll just spit it out: I murdered a man in my youth, Paul."

There was a silence as Paul looked at him, blinking his eyes. A grandfather clock in the hallway inside the front door was ticking, and a few birds flew by on their way home to their nests, but otherwise there was silence. Finally, Paul spoke: "What did you say?"

"I murdered a man. A British officer, name of Charlesworth. I was a boy of 18, and a great anger came over me and somehow I, I hit him. . . I ran away from Ireland because of it. Changed my name. I was born Sean McCarthy, you see, not Peter Morley. I lived in fear always, all my life, that I would be found out. It's been a great weight on me."

"How do I know you're not lying?" Paul said. He seemed unsure, suspicious.

"It's true. I'm not excusing myself, you understand, for what I did to Rose and you boys. I failed you, and that's my responsibility. I just," he bowed his head, "I just wanted to tell someone about this. I've carried it inside for so long." His guts were on fire again, and he clutched at his stomach. It was like some poison was spreading throughout his midsection, a vile brew that was scalding everything it touched. He gasped in pain, holding on to the swing to brace himself.

Paul was unmoved. He stared at James as if he were a specimen under glass in a laboratory. "How did you kill him?" he said.

"I beat him to death," James gasped. "It was an ugly scene. I was just a poor Paddy to them, a nobody, and I don't know, something snapped inside me. I would give anything if it hadn't happened, but it did and I've lived with it every day since. The man even had a son, not much older than yourself, and I met him during the Great War. He was an officer himself, and he was giving a speech in Philadelphia. I robbed that man of his father." He looked at Paul through a veil of tears. "Why, he might even have children now who'll never know their grandfather. I'm glad I got to see my grandchildren today, Paul. Because of me there's a man who never saw his."

"Why are you telling me this?" Paul said, staring coldly at him. "I'm not even sure I believe you. Why tell me?"

"Because I couldn't tell the priest," James said. "And I had to tell someone. That man's spirit was weighing on me my whole life. I had to confess my crime. Maybe you'll understand some day, my boy. I'll be leaving you now." He stood up, but staggered a bit from the pain in his stomach, then grabbed the chain that was attached from the swing to the porch ceiling and righted himself.

"You don't look well enough to leave," Paul said. "It's not that I want you to stay, you understand, but you look like you need to lie down."

"No, no," James said, waving his hand. "It's nothing but a little pain, and I'm used to it. I told that young cab driver to come back here in an hour, and he should be arriving soon. I'll just wait here and—"

His eyes widened once, as if he were staring into eternity, and he fell forward into Paul's arms. Paul tried to hold onto him, but the rocking chair swung backward and James dropped out of his arms and fell on the floor with a thump.

"Father!" Paul said, dropping down to his knees and cradling James in his arms. "Are you all right? Can you hear me?"

James looked up at him through heavy lidded eyes. "Edith," he said, once. Then his body went limp.

CHAPTER NINETEEN

July 3, 1933

There was no record that James Francis belonged to a Catholic church, and at first the pastor at Paul's church did not want to give his permission to bury the old man in consecrated ground. "The man could be a Lutheran for all I know," he said. "You don't even have proof he was baptized."

"He was born in 1862 in Ireland," Paul said. "The record keeping was not the best back then, especially for the poor. He told me he was baptized, and I believe him. Besides, the last conversation I had with him, he said he had just been to Confession." It may have helped that Paul played golf every Saturday with the priest, and that he raised thousands of dollars for the new wing of the grade school, but the man finally relented.

Paul did not mention that his father had had two wives, or that he was known by two names. All that was better left unsaid. He knew he had to contact his father's other wife, however, and any children who might be around. He found an envelope in James's pants pocket addressed to "Edith Francis" at 217B Forsythia Street, Philadelphia. *I wonder if he was carrying that around because he knew he was going to die and he wanted someone to find it on him,* Paul thought.

He went to the address on the envelope, and found it was a room in an apartment building. The woman who answered the door was petite, with gray wavy hair swept back from her forehead, a milky English complexion, and lively gray-green eyes. She was dressed primly in a high-necked brown dress that came to mid-calf and sensible brown shoes.

She seemed unsure about Paul, listening as he explained who he was and why he was here, and when Paul came to the part about how his father was formerly known as Peter Morley she sighed deeply and opened the door to let him in.

Her apartment was tidy, with nothing out of place. She had a small living room with a Chesterfield couch and matching chairs upholstered in a blue fabric with a paisley design, and there was a small walnut coffee table on a blue and red Oriental rug. The walls had pictures of stern-looking men and women staring into the camera, the men in high Victorian collars, and the women sitting at their side in black dresses with voluminous skirts. There was no picture of her husband, Paul noticed.

"Would you like some tea, Mr. Morley?" Edith said. She had a high, fluting voice and a slight English accent, which made her sound like she was always asking a question. She sat on the couch and Paul sat on one of the chairs.

"No thank you," Paul said.

"How did he die?" she asked.

"He came to visit me," Paul said. "I hadn't seen him in years. He wanted to tell me. . . uh, something important. He seemed to be in pain, and he told me it was cancer. It all happened kind of suddenly. . . He just collapsed on my porch and died."

"And you are his son?"

"Yes. He left my mother more than 30 years ago. He was not a part of our lives. That's why I was surprised to see him the other day. I knew very little about his life. . . I didn't know he had married someone else."

There was a long silence. "He kept a lot of secrets, didn't he?" Edith said. Her eyes welled up, and she fought to stay composed. "I don't feel like I ever really knew him."

"None of us did," Paul said. Should he tell her Peter's deepest secret: that he confessed to murdering a man years ago? Would Peter have wanted her to know that?

She was trembling ever so slightly, and her lip was quivering as she fought to control herself. She finally straightened her shoulders and began to speak.

"I was married to him for 15 years," Edith said. "I did not know about his previous marriage. He never told me about that part of his life. When I found out. . . well, at first I found a photograph of a woman and some children. . . it was probably your family, now that I think of it. . . he told me a fable about that picture, that it was a cousin or something. . . I wanted to believe him. Somehow, we survived that crisis, but there were always new ones. He was an attractive man, and he could not resist being carried off by his emotions when it came to women. I could not live like that. We had two children and it was not fair to them, was it?"

"No," Paul said.

"I am sorry I met him," Edith said, with shocking vehemence. "I was only here a short time, and I was going back to England. It changed my life, meeting him. I would have had a different life, if not for that man."

"He hurt a lot of people," Paul said.

"Yes." She stood up. "I thank you for coming here," she said, holding out her hand for Paul to take. "I will not be coming to the funeral, though. I cannot bring myself to do that."

"I understand," Paul said, standing up. "I am sorry I had to bring you this news."

She walked him to the door.

"One thing I think you should know," Paul said, just before going out the door. "The last thing he said was your name."

Edith seemed to rock back on her heels, and her eyes welled up again. She took Paul's hand in hers. "Thank you," she said. "Thank you for telling me that."

Paul put his hand on the doorknob, but she said, "When is the funeral?"

"Tomorrow at 10 in the morning," Paul said. "The church is called St. John of the Cross, in Cheltenham, near where I live. He's going to be buried in a cemetery nearby, called Holy Sepulchre."

He turned to go. "Oh, I almost forgot," he said. "I found this in his pants pocket." He pulled the envelope addressed to her out of his pocket and gave it to her.

Edith looked at the name and address, in James' handwriting, and sighed. "Thank you," she said. "It may be that I will come to the funeral. Goodbye, Mr. Morley."

CHAPTER TWENTY

July 4, 1933

Ah, Sean McCarthy, is it really you lying there?

Rose looked at the face scored with lines, the black hair turned to white, the eyes closed against Life, veiling those pools of ocean blue that had twinkled when he laughed. And where was the laugh now? His mouth was nothing but a sagging line across the bottom of his face. They didn't look like the lips she had kissed so long ago, nor the mouth that had sung "Dear Old Skibbereen" at her American Wake. People in their caskets never looked real to her. Willy and Tim, and all the other people she'd seen die, that wasn't them in Death. It was something else, a sorry copy of Life, a simulacrum, a thing with no heart beating in it.

This was no different. She'd seen him asleep enough times when she was young, and this was not the face she'd looked at next to her in bed.

Only the hands still looked something like him, big hands with surprisingly long, delicate fingers. Hands that had once touched her face ever so gently.

But that was long ago. Those hands had touched another's face since then, and she was here today. Rose looked around and saw his other wife standing in the back of the church, in a plain gray suit, her head uncovered, and at her side were a woman and a man, who must have been her children with Peter. Or James, or whatever he called himself when he married her.

Rose made her way to the pew in the front of the church, next to Martin and Lucy and Paul, and she knelt down and bowed her head. Her mother's voice, which she hadn't heard in so many years, came back, whispering:

"This is the fruit of believing in this heartless world, my darling. Destruction, decay, and death are all it holds for us. We must escape to another world, a better one. A world where everyone is happy, where the fairies dance the night away under the full moon, while the forest animals watch them as if in a dream. It is a world. . ."

"Enough!" Rose hissed. Her voice echoed in the old stone church, but she did not care. She had banished her mother once before, had not heard the voice in years, but now the old woman was trying to come back, although her voice was weak. Rose wanted no parts of her. I am stronger now, she thought. It was an easy matter to excise her forever from Rose's mind.

She turned to see the other woman, whose name was Edith, Paul had told her, coming up the aisle just before the casket was closed. She was a small woman with small facial features, though attractive in a prim, fine-boned way. She was supported by her daughter and son, and she seemed so shaky that they were almost carrying her. She paused in front of the casket and a tear rolled down her cheek, although she made no sound. She put her hand on the cold cheek of her husband, and then she bent down and kissed him. Rose realized in that moment that this woman had truly loved the man she had loved, and that she loved a different man than Rose did. He gave us all pieces of his soul, Rose thought. Like a man dividing up a pie.

Her heart opened to Edith, realizing that they shared something precious. Their hearts had endured the storm of loving this man, and they were forever changed by it. At least I have found Martin, Rose thought. I have come out of the storm into the safe harbor of Martin's arms. It looks like Edith has no one else.

The air was cool inside the stone church, but when they carried the casket out the atmosphere was heavy and humid, and the sky was low with clouds. The rain had not come for a month, even though it had threatened for many days, and the city was choking on the humidity.

There were only a handful of mourners besides Rose and Paul's family, and Edith and her grown children. A few Irish that remembered Peter from his days singing in saloons, and had read the obituary in the newspaper were all that came to say goodbye to the man who was once known as Sean McCarthy.

Rose wondered if he still had family back in Ireland. Did he have a mother or a father still alive? Sisters or brothers? Did they ever wonder what became of him? He had never told her anything about his family. "It's all in the past," he'd say. "Not worth talking about, my darling."

She wondered if she should say anything to Edith, but Paul hurried her into his car and she did not have the chance. At the cemetery, they walked over dry, broken ground to the gravesite, and the priest said some brief prayers and then an altar boy offered Rose a red rose to throw on the casket before it was lowered into the ground. She threw it, then the boy offered one to Paul, but he shook his head no. Edith was standing in the back of the small crowd, but she did not move.

Rose took one of the flowers and made her way back to Edith. She handed it to her and said, "Perhaps you want this."

"Thank you," Edith said, then went forward and threw the rose onto the casket.

When the ceremony was over, Paul took Rose's arm and tried to guide her back to his car, but she pulled away from him and Martin and walked over to Edith, who was weeping in the arms of her daughter.

"I am sorry for your grief," Rose said. She took Edith's

hand in hers. "He was a scoundrel, but he was unforgettable, to be sure."

"Thank you," Edith said, holding her hand tightly. "I know you were his first wife. I found a picture of you and your children once, long ago. You still look the same."

"Ah," Rose said. "The picture. I don't know why I had it taken. I hoped it would make him love us more, I suppose."

"I would not tolerate his deceit," Edith said, wiping her tears away. "I threw him out of my life. I regret that now. I wish I had been kinder to him. My heart is broken."

"We do what we think is right at the time," Rose said. "Do not regret it. You have wonderful memories of him, I am sure. And he gave you two children. Life goes on. I can see him in the faces of your children. He lives on in that way." She turned to go, then said: "You will find love again, I believe that. It is possible, because it happened to me."

She turned to Martin, who, as always, was by her side. "Let us go now, Martin. I promised little Rose and Billy I'd take tea with them this afternoon."

There was a far off rumble of thunder, and then a gentle rain began to fall.

ROSE OF SKIBBEREEN - (Book 2)

...THE END OF BOOK TWO

This is the second of the seven books in the Rose Of Skibbereen series. Look for the other books on Amazon at: amazon.com/author/johnmcdonnell.

A word from John McDonnell:

I have been a writer all my life, but after many years of doing other types of writing I'm finally returning to my first love, which is fiction. The new world of digital publishing has changed my life, as it has for thousands of other writers. I have published more than a dozen works of fiction and poetry in the last few years, and I have plans to publish lots more. I write in the horror, sci-fi, romance, humor and fantasy genres. I like them all! I also write plays, and I have a YouTube channel where I post some of them. I live near Philadelphia, Pennsylvania with my wife and four children, and I am a happy man.

My books on Amazon:
amazon.com/author/johnmcdonnell.

My YouTube channel:
https://www.youtube.com/user/McDonnellWrite/videos

Look me up on Facebook at:
https://www.facebook.com/JohnMcDonnellsWriting

Did you like this book? Did you enjoy the characters? Do you have any advice you'd like to give me? Do you want to know when the next "Rose Of Skibbereen" book will be coming out? I love getting feedback on my books. Send me an email at: mcdonnellwrite@gmail.com.

Printed in Great Britain
by Amazon